JESSIE

Linda Bolté Whitlock

ISBN: 1499121210
ISBN 13: 9781499121216
Library of Congress Control Number: 2014920319
CreateSpace Independent Publishing Platform
North Charleston, South Carolina

Jessie Willard Bolté

We always called Jessie "Byma." I knew her through our two winter
trips to Florida and her visits to us in Greenwich, Connecticut.
I knew she had to wear a brace on her right leg, and she had
a thick sole on her right shoe and a funny walk. She was quite
strict about table manners, and she played the piano—vigorously.
But I did not know anything else about her, really, until I read
Uncle Willy's family history, *Bolté Memoirs and Genealogy*. That
book made me realize what a courageous woman Jessie was. I
dedicate her story to my descendants and, of course, to hers.

For my children, grandchildren,
and great-grandchildren,
and any who come in future generations.

CONTENTS

CHAPTER ONE

W hy can't I move? Maybe I am dead. It is so dark. Are my eyes open? Yes, but there is no light. I do not hear anything either. I rub my eyes. Oh! My arms and hands still work. The right leg never works, so it's just the left leg that is different. I reach down with my left hand and feel plaster. I groan. Plaster can only mean that I have broken that leg again. Why can't I remember breaking it? And did I break my head too? It aches.

The door opens—not my door. It's in the wrong place. There is light beyond it, and I hear voices. The figure outlined in the doorway wears a nurse's cap. She comes in softly and turns on a small lamp beside my bed.

"You're awake," she says, smiling. "How do you feel?"

"My head hurts and I can't move my leg, but I don't remember what happened. Did I fall?"

"Yes. You slipped at your son's house. You broke your leg and hit your head hard enough to knock you out but not hard enough to break it. It's not surprising that you don't remember. That often happens with a head injury. You also were given quite a lot of ether while your leg was being set, and that might have affected your memory. Are you thirsty? Would you like a cup of tea?"

I realize I am very thirsty. "Yes please, with sugar but no cream or lemon." The nurse goes out, and I close my eyes. I drift back to my childhood.

I am lying on a blanket on the dining room table. My father is sitting in a chair beside me, reading a paper. I can't move my legs, but he keeps saying I have to try. I am so angry I am crying, banging my head and my fists on the table. He takes both of my fists in his right hand and holds my head down with his left.

"Stop crying," he says.

Gulping and sniffling, I say, "May I get down now please?"

"No. Exercising your head and arms isn't going to do any good. You have to move those legs. Now try again."

I try so hard to move the right one that I stop breathing, but nothing happens. My eyes fill with tears again.

"Don't cry," he says, "and try again."

I try with all my might to move the left leg and suddenly feel that it's off the blanket. My father shouts, "Yes!" and calls my mother, who is in the kitchen. "Wait until you see what Jessie can do," he says.

Coming into the dining room, she bends over and gives me a hug. "Show me," she says, smiling.

I take a deep breath, push down with my hands, and lift my left foot a whole inch off the table. My mother, half laughing and half crying, scoops me up and carries me into the living room.

Even tonight, sixty years later, I have a vivid memory of that scene, though I was only three years old. I can feel the hard table, my rage at

Father, and the triumph of being able to lift that left foot, even so little. I don't remember the preceding illness at all. Only after I had children of my own did I realize what a hard time it must have been for my parents. They told me about it later.

My screaming had awakened my mother in the middle of the night. My symptoms were headache, vomiting, a fever of 105, and then diarrhea. After five days, I began to ache all over, especially in my neck. I was weak, becoming weaker, and within a few hours was paralyzed from the waist down. It was hard to move my arms but not impossible. Dr. Adams, who had brought me into the world and who took care of all of us for many years, did not know what was wrong with me until I became paralyzed.

Nobody knew much about polio in 1858, though the discovery of some ancient Egyptian mummies with one leg shorter than the other suggested that the disease existed long ago. According to a physician visiting Louisiana in 1841, the illness was related to teething, but some years after I got it, after the Civil War, epidemics began to be reported from European and American cities indicating that older children and young adults were also susceptible.

One of the mercies of life is that we don't really remember physical pain. I have no recollection of that early pain, but I remember the house we lived in. It was on South Wabash Avenue in Chicago. My parents, Alonzo and Laura Willard, had moved into it right after their wedding in 1855. The square house was three stories high, with no cellar but with a porch extending around the corner on the south side. I played on that porch in bad weather, winter and summer, to get what my father called my "daily dose of fresh air." We had a big yard with hedges between our neighbors and us. Along the street was a picket fence painted tan to match the trim of the otherwise dark brown house. I remember struggling to open the heavy, carved front door, which led to an entrance hall with two archways. The left one opened onto the living room and thence to the study; the right opened to the dining room, with the butler's pantry, kitchen, and laundry room beyond. The floors in the living area were covered with large Oriental rugs, predominantly red, but the broad stairs were uncarpeted.

The second floor consisted of five bedrooms with a bathroom at the end of the hall. South Wabash Avenue had city water and had recently been connected to the new sewer system. Gaslights had been installed on the street in 1850, but in the house we still had to use oil lamps and candles. We had two guest rooms and two servant's rooms on the third floor. The rest of the floor, unfinished, was used for storage.

Most of the house was dark, not only because of the limited illumination but also because of the rugs and the dark, heavy drapes on the floor-length windows. The only bright room was mine. As it was on the southeast corner of the house, it got more sunlight than any other room. The doctor asked that my heavy curtains be removed as soon as my fever went down. That's when my exercise schedule began too. Three times a day one of my parents or one of the maids put me on the dining table and gave me passive exercises, moving each of my four limbs Then I was supposed to try to move them myself. And how I hated those sessions! I never gave a thought to what a trial they were to the people working on me—never, that is, until one particularly bad time.

Addie, one of our two Negro maids, was in charge of my afternoon exercises that day. Some of the procedures were painful, and halfway through I began to scream. "You're hurting me! You can't do that! You're just a bad maid!" When Addie bent down to continue, I scratched her face and shouted, "Go away! Get away from me!" Addie left. Still on the dining room table, I fell asleep. My father found me there when he came home from the office. I opened my eyes and turned away from him.

"You've been crying again," he said accusingly. "I've told you and told you that you mustn't cry. Now what have you done? Why have you been left here alone?"

"I hate Addie," I said, trying not to cry again.

"That's no answer." He strode into the kitchen calling Addie. I heard him say, "Jessie did that, didn't she. What happened?"

Addie told him, adding, "She didn' mean nothin' by it. She jist a baby an' she in pain."

"She has to learn to think about other people," he said, and he strode back to the dining room. "You know Addie wasn't trying to hurt you, don't you?"

I nodded.

"You know that she and Janie are working just as hard as your mother and I are to help you get better?"

I nodded again.

"You've been having a terrible time, and it's not over yet. Even Dr. Adams doesn't know when it will be. But at least you don't hurt as much as you used to, do you?"

"Just sometimes."

"Today was a bad day?"

I nodded once more.

"I'm sorry," he said. "You must realize that when you hurt, we all hurt too. Can you understand that?"

I shook my head.

"Well, you will. Now I want you to apologize to Addie. You hurt her face and her feelings, and that you must never do, especially to someone who's trying to help you. I'll get her."

I didn't want to apologize. I wanted to hide, but I couldn't get off the table. When Addie came in with her arms out, however, I held mine out too, and as we hugged each other, I whispered, "I'm sorry."

My father was a stern man, and while I never had any doubt that he loved me, it was years before I understood why he was so strict with me. He was afraid that I would become a very spoiled little girl, because my illness made me the center of so much attention. More important, he knew I would be lame throughout my life, and he hoped to make me strong enough mentally and emotionally to meet the problems I would face. Most of my life I have been grateful to him, but I remember many nights in my childhood when I cried myself to sleep, biting on the sheet so no one would hear me.

My father, Alonzo Joseph Willard, red-haired and six feet three inches tall, left Wilton, Maine, for Chicago in 1839. At that time there were only twenty-four states, and Illinois was the farthest west. Most of the West beyond still belonged to the Spaniards of Mexico. Father once said he had left New England because "there had been plenty of poverty-stricken teachers and preachers and farmers in the family, and it was time somebody made some money for a change."

It took him a number of years to find out how to do that. After working for a time as a porter in a tavern, he helped build houses. He next worked on a canal boat on the Illinois and Michigan Canal. Eventually he became captain of the boat, and still later he owned several canal boats. He finally started the second ice business in Chicago, cutting ice in the winter on Lake Calumet or Geneva Lake and storing it in great icehouses for the summer trade. On the hottest days, Father would take me and my little brother, Johnny, who was born when I was five, to cool off in one of those icehouses. We would see who could sit the longest on one of the sawdust-covered blocks of ice.

Laura Anne Walter, my mother, was about a foot shorter than my father and a good deal gentler, though she had an inner strength that supported us all. Born in Goshen, Connecticut, she came to Chicago to visit a cousin. She met my father and married him two months later. She used to tell Johnny and me about Connecticut—especially about the beauty of the fall foliage—but she never went back.

When my left leg became strong enough to bear my weight, Dr. Adams gave me a pair of crutches. They were made of heavy wood, but they gave me a new freedom. For more than a year I had had to be carried or pushed in a small chair specially fitted with wheels. Mother was very nervous as I was learning to use the crutches. I did fall a few times at first but only once seriously. A crutch slipped as I was coming down the stairs. There was a terrible clatter as the crutches and I slid down the rest of the way. I remember lying at the bottom, looking up at the frightened faces of my mother, Addie, and Janie. I didn't cry. I let them help me up and hand me the crutches and then went on my way. I had found I could go pretty fast by giving an extra hop with my left leg after each swing through with the crutches.

My father took me to New York when I was five to be fitted with a steel brace, which supported my right leg enough to bear my weight. Since it held my leg stiff, I had to swing to the left to move it forward, and it came down with a clunk on the heel. Everyone always knew when I was coming. I still wasn't able to run, but at least I was rid of the crutches.

That was the year Johnny was born. At first he was red and scrawny and screamed a lot, but I liked him. I liked helping to give him a bath. One day, our neighbor Mrs. Peabody came to visit Mother and see the baby. I was just going into Mother's room to help show off Johnny when

I heard Mrs. Peabody exclaim, "Oh, isn't he beautiful! A boy, and with such nice strong legs! Now you have a child you can really be proud of!" I sat down on the hall rug, and using my hands and my left foot, I pushed myself backward to my room. I didn't want to be heard, and I certainly didn't want to hear any more. I missed my mother's reply, but Mrs. Peabody soon went briskly down the stairs and slammed the door on her way out.

Strange, the things one remembers. Of course Mrs. Peabody hurt my feelings, but it was such a trivial event to last more than fifty years. Maybe I remember it because it was so unusual. People were generally so kind and considerate—much nicer than I sometimes was myself.

The nurse has brought my tea and a hypodermic. Her name is Grace, she says, and after giving me the morphine, she cradles my head on her arm and feeds me the tea, a spoonful at a time. I feel myself relaxing and soon fall asleep.

CHAPTER TWO

I sleep for several hours before the pain in my leg wakes me up. It is not so severe that I need to call the nurse. Instead, I resume my thoughts about my childhood.

Abraham Lincoln has always been one of my heroes, though my father didn't think much of him when he was nominated in 1860. Father admitted later that he thought Abe was just an uncouth backwoods lawyer who had no intention of forbidding slavery in the states, though he thought it should be prohibited in the territories. I didn't know anything about that at the time, since I was only four in 1860, but I did know the word *abolitionist*. Father was one, and he expressed his opinion freely whenever guests came to call.

I didn't know much about the Civil War either, until the day I found my mother crying over John's crib. "What's the matter?" I asked. "Does Father say it's all right for you to cry?"

Mother sat on a low chair and put her arm around me. "I think he would this time," she said. "Do you remember your cousin George?"

"Of course. He gave me a ride on the horse." I had met him and his two younger sisters in June 1860, when Father had taken a week's vacation with Mother and me. I was shy with the cousins at first, but George took charge of me. He carried me all around the farm to show me the animals. I liked the horses best, especially a small mare named Bridget.

I even got to ride her, with George holding me on and his sisters leading her around the pasture.

"You do remember," said Mother. "George went off to join the army. He was killed in the Battle of Shiloh about a month ago. I've just heard about it from your Uncle Haven."

"You mean we'll never see George again?"

Mother shook her head, and I hugged her tighter.

Father used to take us in the family carriage to watch the parades of soldiers, soldiers not only from Illinois but also from Wisconsin, Minnesota, and Iowa. It was exciting to watch them marching along with flags flying and a drummer boy at the head of each company. One day Father took me to see a friend of his who owned a farm a few miles beyond Chicago's city limits. Without intending to, he drove past Camp Douglas, which had been turned into a detention center for Confederate prisoners of war—as many as ten thousand of them at a time. From the road, men, tents, and campfires were visible through the barbed wire fence.

"Are those soldiers?" I asked.

"Yes," said Father, "Southern soldiers who have been captured and are being held prisoner."

"They look just like ours, only their uniforms are all dirty and ragged, and they look cold."

"I'm sure they are. We can just hope and pray that the war will end soon so they can all go home."

Remembering Cousin George and those wretched prisoners has made me hate war ever since, and now my own son is fighting in France.

I pray that this will really turn out to be the war to end war. At least the slaves were finally freed by the Civil War. Addie and Janie were so happy when Father brought home a copy of the Emancipation Proclamation and read it to them. Addie, who was primarily responsible for John and me, rarely cooked, but that night she helped Janie prepare a celebratory feast. Beaming, they both came into the dining room to present Addie's three-layer raisin-nut cake.

"Why are you so happy?" I asked curiously. "You're not slaves. My father would never keep slaves."

Addie spoke first. "You right. We the lucky ones, but we care about those still slaves."

"And we both still got kin among 'em," said Janie. "My mama and three brothers are somewhere way south in Alabama."

"And my daddy's two brothers are in Louisiana. They families been sold, so they don' know where anybody is."

It had never occurred to me that Addie and Janie might have families of their own, much less that those relatives might still be slaves. "Will they be freed right away?" I asked.

Father shook his head. "Unfortunately no. We can't expect the Confederacy to pay any attention to the proclamations of a country with which they are at war. That proclamation makes the whole purpose of the war clearer, however."

I thought it did too. I wish I had as clear a sense of the purpose of the present war—a "world war" it's being called. "A crusade," President Wilson calls it, "to make the world safe for democracy." Well, I hope it does, but I have the unhappy feeling that war seldom solves anything—though it did eventually free all the slaves.

The Civil War was still being fought when I started school. I was eight, and I already knew how to read. I had read and reread *The Pilgrim's Progress, Robinson Crusoe, Gulliver's Travels*, and parts of the Bible. Mother had given me *David Copperfield*, and she and I were reading it together during John's afternoon naps. I knew my numbers and could add and subtract. I could have gone to a public school since public education had come to Chicago by that time, but Mother was concerned about my going to a place with so many children, especially with bigger, older boys. She was afraid I would be knocked over in the halls or teased. There was a small private school for about thirty girls only a few blocks from our house, however. On the recommendation of her friend Mary Cox, whose daughters attended the Ashby School, Mother agreed I should go.

I had met the Cox girls, Sarah and Anne, a few times when their mother came to call on mine. It wasn't much fun to play with them though. They were older than I, and they didn't seem to like me—at least Annie didn't. One day I found out why. We had been playing in my room and all of a sudden Annie got red in the face.

"You're going to have a miserable time in school," she stormed at me, "if you don't stop being so bossy and selfish. You don't own the world, you know!" And she stamped out of my room to find her mother.

I was startled. "Am I really so bossy?" I asked Sarah. Sarah was thirteen and could be expected to know most things.

"Well, yes, you are," said Sarah slowly. "I guess you haven't played with many children besides Johnny, and he's too little to fight back—aren't you, Johnny?" She picked him up and swung him, laughing, high above her head.

She and Annie were right. Despite my father's best efforts, I had become an imperious little girl, given to ordering other people around and certain that I was always right. And I'm afraid I've never fully overcome those flaws in my character.

I was not feeling imperious or certain about anything as the opening day of school approached, however. I was impatient, but I was also increasingly nervous. I knew I was different, not only because I was lame but also because, as Sarah Cox said, I had not played with many other children. I was afraid I would never have any friends. Father drove me to school the first morning. I didn't tell him how nervous I was, but he seemed to know.

"You'll be fine," he murmured as he helped me down from the carriage and gave me a swift hug. He led me up the shallow steps to the open double doors of the old brownstone building that had once been the Ashbys' house. Just inside stood the Misses Hodge, the founders and principal teachers of the school. Helen, the older and bigger one known as Miss Hodge, was the headmistress and took charge of the older girls; Miss Fanny was in charge of the younger ones. Both taught English, mathematics, history, and geography. Miss Hodge taught elocution to all classes. Miss Alicia Conti taught art, music, and French; she was the daughter of a Chicago heiress who had married an Italian.

There were two other new girls, and Miss Hodge introduced us to the whole school at the opening day assembly. I'll never forget her additional remarks about me: "When Jessie was a little girl, she became dreadfully sick, and her sickness left her with a crippled leg. She gets around very well with a brace, but she cannot run and play as the rest of you can. I know that you will all be very kind and helpful to her." Then she asked me to stand up. I wished that I could disappear through the floor—or better yet, prove the fat Miss Hodge wrong by running out of the assembly room. I could feel myself blushing as I sat down.

After the assembly, we younger students were led to our own room at the end of the building. I was assigned a desk in the middle row, a desk that remained mine for the next four years. Miss Fanny, the thin Hodge, asked Anne Cox and Elsie Martin to hand out the readers, which contained material that was supposed to be appropriate for young ladies aged seven to eleven. To my relief, Anne gave me a friendly smile when she handed me my book.

I kept quiet for the first week or so at Ashby, watching and listening. I found I could read and understand everything in the reader, and I knew about the same amount of arithmetic and history as the other eight-year-olds, but I didn't know any French while the others had already had it for a year. I always waited to be at the end of the line when the class moved to Miss Conti's room or the lavatory or the dining room. I didn't want to hold the others up or be stared at. I was beginning to feel less self-conscious until the day I arrived a few minutes later than usual, though classes hadn't started yet. I went to the cloakroom to hang up my coat, and there were my three classmates. They were obviously practicing my walk, single file, with their backs to the door. They didn't see me as they staggered, giggling, toward the end of the narrow room.

Hurt and angry at first, I didn't know what to do. I just stood in the doorway for a moment, but then I began to laugh. "No, no!" I said. "You're doing it all wrong! Come on, I'll show you." I tossed my coat on a hook, turned back to the doorway, and led my classmates rocking and clunking down the hall to Miss Fanny's room.

CHAPTER THREE

B y the middle of that first year, I felt that I belonged at Ashby. I had
made friends with my three mimics and with several of the older
girls. I seldom thought about my lame leg, which was hidden under the
long skirts of the current style, and my friends had come to take it for
granted. Best of all, I was getting to know Miss Conti, the third teacher
at Ashby.

Alicia Conti, who was in her early twenties, had studied art and
music in Italy. Tall and graceful, with wavy dark brown hair and brown
eyes, she was everything that I wished to be—and the opposite of what
I was. A singer herself, she directed the school choir and tested every
new student for membership. Having learned a number of songs from
Mother and Janie during my physical therapy sessions, I liked to sing.
I had an accurate sense of pitch and a clear voice, though by no means
a great one. After I had sung two songs for the test, Miss Conti enrolled
me in the choir as a soprano. Then she took me to the grand piano in the
corner of the music room. I had attended several piano concerts, and I
had seen Mrs. Cox's upright piano, which children were not allowed
to touch. Consequently I had never played a note. Miss Conti played a
simple tune and then invited me to try.

"Perhaps you would like to learn to play," she said after I had tenta-
tively struck a few notes.

"Oh! Do you think I could?" I couldn't reach the pedal with my left foot, but I liked the sound.

"We'll try a few lessons and see."

That was Miss Conti's first great gift to me. She gave me some lessons at school and then called on my parents to persuade Father to buy me a piano. He liked the idea, and Mother, who was very musical, was particularly pleased. For the next three years, Miss Conti came to the house each Saturday morning to give me a lesson. I never became a concert pianist (though I had that dream for a time), but I did become the school pianist, playing for the other students as they marched into assemblies and accompanying the morning hymns as well as school musical performances.

Miss Conti's other great gift was teaching me to ride a horse. Her mother had inherited a large estate on what had been the outskirts of Chicago, though the city was already encroaching on the property. Miss Conti's grandfather had been especially proud of his stable, his two matched carriage teams, and his eighteen riding horses. He saw to it that his granddaughter learned to ride almost before she learned to walk. When the Civil War began and the army was scouring the countryside for horses, his wife donated twelve. One of the carriage teams had already been retired. She kept the other for her own use, and she put Alicia in charge of the remaining six riding horses. When the two stable boys enlisted in the army, the head groom said the horses had to have more riders. Alicia knew that some of her students were already experienced riders and some had, like her grandmother, sacrificed horses to the army. When Alicia proposed the Ashby Riding Club, Miss Hodge approved. Nine students responded eagerly.

Alicia rode every day after school, and at first she took only experienced riders with her. She was eventually persuaded, however, to start a class for beginners. One Saturday morning, after my weekly piano lesson, she looked at me speculatively.

"I don't suppose you've ever been on a horse, have you?"

"Oh yes!" I said. "My cousin George, the one who was killed in the war, gave me a ride all around his father's farm."

"Did you like it?"

"It was wonderful!"

"You weren't afraid of the horse?"

"No. Bridget was very gentle, and anyway George held me on while his sisters led her."

"Would you like to learn to ride properly?"

I had never imagined such a possibility. "Could I? I mean, do you think I would be able to stay on alone?"

"I think you could with the right kind of saddle. Let's talk to your parents and see what they think."

Mother was filled with trepidation at the prospect, but Father was enthusiastic. He wanted me to do whatever my peers did, whenever possible. Mother insisted on discussing the proposal with Dr. Adams, who in turn discussed it with Alicia and her head groom. They decided that both the horse and I would be better off without my brace and that I should use a sidesaddle with two pommels, one on either side of my right leg, to protect it and to make me feel secure. Mother was still much concerned about what would happen if I should fall off and be dragged by my horse.

"She just mustn't fall off," Father said cheerfully.

Miss Conti was more practical. "The horse I have in mind is so well trained and so gentle that he would stop instantly if she should fall off."

My first few lessons were private, with Miss Conti instructing and Fred Hill, the groom, leading me on Hector, the well-trained horse. I was ecstatic. On Hector I felt equal to anyone, and I soon gained enough skill and confidence to join the regular beginners' class, held Tuesdays after school.

During my first term at Ashby, Abraham Lincoln was reelected. Father, encouraged by the fall of Atlanta to Sherman in early September and hopeful that the end of the war might finally be in sight, decided to support the president and actively campaigned for him in Illinois. Father was ready to do anything he could to prevent McClellan from being elected and restoring slavery. When the Thirteenth Amendment, which completely abolished slavery in the United States, was passed on January 31, 1865, we all rejoiced. After Lee surrendered at Appomattox on April 9, Alicia Conti organized a parade of all the riders who still had horses or could borrow horses on the north side of Chicago. In school we made red, white, and blue rosettes for the horses' bridles and banners for the riders to carry. I rode Hector.

And then on the night of April 14, President Lincoln was shot. He died the next morning. When Miss Hodge heard the news, she called us all together for a special assembly. She tried, but there was no way she could lessen the shock to all of us. We had been so happy less than a week ago. The war was all but over, wasn't it? I couldn't understand how it could have happened—or why. And it has never seemed fair that he was shot just as the war was ending.

The funeral train went from Washington to New York and then west. The girls at Ashby decided to join the other Chicago schoolchildren in the procession across the city, and of course I wanted to march too.

"You can't!" Mother protested. "You'll be exhausted after three blocks!"

Seeing how determined I was, Father said, "Why don't you ride Hector? I'm sure Miss Conti would agree, and that way you could pay your respects to the president without getting too tired."

I remember having trouble explaining. "It would be just too easy to ride Hector," I finally said. So I became one of the ten thousand schoolchildren, wearing black armbands, who followed Lincoln's coffin through the streets of Chicago. A fine gesture on my part, perhaps, but certainly a foolish one. My mother was perfectly right. I couldn't walk more than three blocks, and those three blocks gave me a large blister where the brace rubbed my thigh. I sat on the curb watching the other children go by, trying not to cry, until Father came along in the carriage. He said he had wanted to be a part of the procession, but I suspect he knew I would need help.

I suppose it is always hard to recognize one's own limitations—and harder still to accept them. I was too often stubborn about mine. But it is so frustrating not to be able to do what one wants to do! Right now, for instance, I want to get up and walk out of this hospital, but I can't even turn myself over. The sun is coming up, however. It must be almost time for breakfast. I will try to be patient and uncomplaining. Huh! I can hear my sons laughing at that idea!

CHAPTER FOUR

Soon after breakfast and a sponge bath, carefully administered by Dorothy, the morning nurse, I am visited by my son Willard and his wife, whose name, like mine, is Jessie. That coincidence has elicited some tasteless jokes about how Willard wanted to marry his mother, but young Jess, as we call her, is not the least bit like me. She is highly independent and brooks no interference from anybody. She and Willard now have three little boys of their own. When the first one, John, was born, of course I had some helpful suggestions for Jess, but she wanted no part of them—and made her feelings quite clear. Ever since then I have been trying to learn to keep my opinions to myself, but I admit it's a struggle. I have developed considerable respect for Jess, however—more, I'm afraid, than for Guy's wife, though I do feel sorry for poor Mary.

Jess is full of contrition. "Are you all right, Mother Bolté? I feel terrible about your fall. It was all my fault—I never should have had the floor waxed when I knew you were coming. I've never been so frightened in my life as when I saw you lying on the floor, not moving."

"How do you feel, Mother?" asks Willard. "The boys were scared to death too. They wanted to come and see you, but I said not today. You look pale. Are you really all right?"

"Quite all right," I say firmly, "though I am tired."

They take the hint and stay only a few more minutes. There is no need to tell them I am also in pain. This is the second time I've broken my left leg at their house. The first time, I tripped over a scatter rug. Perhaps after this I better just stay in Winnetka. Let them come to me rather than my going to Indianapolis. Dorothy brings me another hypo, and I drift back to the Ashby School.

At the end of my third year, Miss Conti left Ashby to be married to an army officer. I thought that was highly romantic, but I could hardly bear to think of the school without her. We gave her a going away party in June, shortly before her wedding. I helped Addie make one of her special raisin-nut cakes, and other students provided little tea sandwiches, cupcakes, and lemonade. Miss Hodge gave a lengthy farewell speech in which she made clear her opinion that a teaching career was far more laudable than a matrimonial one. She presented Miss Conti with the school's wedding gift, an ormolu mantel clock. A number of students also gave gifts, and the choir sang two songs we had rehearsed secretly. I thought of writing a song, but I couldn't get the words to match my feelings, so instead I wrote a waltz and played it at the end of the party. As Miss Conti was leaving, girls crowded around her, some of them in tears. I stayed by the piano. I was determined not to cry, and I couldn't think of anything to say. After the other girls left, Miss Conti walked over to me.

"The waltz was beautiful," she said. "Thank you. You are one student I know I won't forget. If I write you, will you answer?"

I nodded.

"I have no idea where I'll be five years from now. You never know when you marry an army officer. But if it's possible, perhaps you could visit me after you graduate. Would you come?"

"Oh yes, please," I said. Miss Conti kissed me good-bye, and I swung quickly out of the room.

The following fall, when I was twelve, I moved from Miss Fanny's room to Miss Hodge's larger one at the front of the building. Since there were only thirty-four students attending Ashby, we all knew one another. My closest friend was Margaret Ames. We were direct opposites: she was tall and fair while I was dark and still quite short. We always sat together in class—except when we were separated for whispering or giggling. Maggie was an excellent rider, and on Saturday morning we rode together in Lincoln Park, now that Miss Conti was gone.

I suppose to some extent Kay Woodward replaced Miss Conti that year. A senior, Kay led the school in just about everything: intelligence, musical talent, looks, and humor. Unlike some of the other older girls, she was always friendly and kind to younger students. There was a time that year when I was really depressed. Maggie and our other two classmates, Elizabeth Maher and Jane Phelps, had all begun to mature physically, and I had not. They called me a baby, whispered together in corners, and stopped when I came near. They all began to be interested in boys. I used to think that I would never become a real woman, that nobody would ever want to marry me, and that I would never be able to have children. I had met a few brothers of Ashby girls and didn't like them much. The only boy I knew well was Johnny, and he was still something of a pest.

Hurt and lonely, I daydreamed about performing heroic acts: of racing after Maggie's runaway horse and saving her just before her horse plunged over the precipice; of dragging Maggie and Elizabeth and Jane from a burning building; of diving into Lake Michigan to rescue Kay Woodward. Then not only my three classmates but the whole school would appreciate me too. I started spending my free time practicing the piano in the auditorium and wishing Miss Conti were still there. Miss Eliot, the new music teacher, was a stiff, middle-aged woman who could not keep discipline in her classes. We all made fun of her behind her back.

One day, just as I was finishing "None But the Lonely Heart," I realized someone else had come into the auditorium and sat down. I stopped playing and turned to see Kay Woodward sitting in one of the senior chairs.

"Don't stop," she said. "I like to hear you play. What's the name of that piece?"

Reluctantly I told her, and Kay nodded.

"It sounds like its title," she said. "You've been feeling a bit lonely yourself lately, haven't you?"

I was astonished. "How did you know?" I asked.

"It's such a small school you can't help seeing what's happening to everybody else if you pay attention."

"Not many people pay attention though," I said a little bitterly, "especially to babies like me."

"You'd be surprised. My friends and I all have a lot of respect for you. We admire you for your courage and your talent and the fact that you don't waste time feeling sorry for yourself. And we certainly don't think of you as a baby."

I could feel myself blushing. "I guess I've been feeling pretty sorry for myself lately," I said.

"Why?"

"My friends all think they're so grown up and I'm just a baby because I don't...I haven't—" I stopped.

"Because you haven't caught up to them physically?"

I nodded.

"There's nothing wrong with you except that your leg is paralyzed, is there?"

"No, at least not that I know of. The doctor says I'm normal."

"Well then, you just have to be patient. Your friends are being silly, but they'll get over that. It's a hard age, twelve to fourteen, and sometimes a cruel one." Kay paused reflectively. "People seem to get nicer at sixteen or seventeen. Next time you're feeling lonesome, come talk to me and my friends." She smiled and waved as she headed for the door. "I hope you'll play for me again."

"Oh yes," I breathed, smiling as I know I hadn't smiled for weeks. I didn't feel alone anymore. Now whenever I felt left out, I remembered Kay's words. I did talk to her and her friends occasionally, but I was too shy and afraid of becoming a nuisance to do it often. I was sad when Kay graduated from Ashby, but by that time Maggie and I were good friends again.

In the next three years I caught up to my classmates and even grew a few inches. I was still the shortest, but at least no one called me "baby" anymore. In the spring of our form three year, I had the bright idea of putting on a show based on Ashby people and events. I wish I had never thought of it. I wrote two songs, and each of the four of us wrote a skit. Mine was a parody of one of Miss Eliot's classes. Maggie warned me that it might not be very well received, but Elizabeth and Jane thought it was so funny, and I was such a good mimic of Miss Eliot that we decided to risk it. Miss Hodge agreed to let us present the show at a Friday afternoon all-school assembly. The program was to begin and end with one of my songs, and mine was the last skit. Parents were invited to attend.

The audience laughed and clapped enthusiastically at the first three skits but was silent at the beginning of mine. We went on anyway, and soon the students burst out laughing. I didn't see Miss Eliot leave the auditorium, but my mother did. After the last song, she came over to the piano and gave me a quick hug, but she was not smiling. Miss Hodge came up right behind her.

"I want to see you in my office now, Jessie," said Miss Hodge, "before you go home. Perhaps you will come too, Mrs. Willard?"

"Of course," said my mother.

We walked out of the auditorium and across the hall to Miss Hodge's office. She closed the door.

"Sit down," she said, though she remained standing behind her desk. "I am ashamed of you, Jessie, and I am personally humiliated. Making a mockery of one of my teachers makes a mockery of the Ashby School and consequently of me because the school is my life. I thought you were happy here, that you liked Ashby."

I started to say something, but she held up her hand.

"Just let me finish," she said. "You spoiled an otherwise amusing and entertaining program. I'm afraid you're too clever for your own good. I didn't think you needed to be censored, but today's was certainly the last such performance I shall ever allow. I have not decided what your school punishment will be, but I'm glad your mother was here. She will know how to deal with you at home. That is all that needs to be said now." She crossed the room, opened the door, and stood there, waiting for us to leave.

When I started to speak again, Mother gently took my hand and led me out of the room and the school to our carriage.

"All that woman ever thinks of is her precious Ashby School!" I stormed impenitently on the way home.

"That was my impression too," said Mother. "She completely overlooked the real tragedy of the afternoon."

"Tragedy?" I didn't know what she was talking about.

"If you had seen Miss Eliot's face, you might understand what I mean. I'd like you to go to your room when we get home and think about her. We'll talk when your father gets home."

I confess that I hadn't given one minute's thought to the effect of that wretched skit on Miss Eliot. I squirm now when I think of it, but I was still feeling defensive when my father came home and called me downstairs. He led me into the library where he sat behind his desk. Mother and I sat in the matching wing chairs in front of him.

"Your mother has told me there was some trouble at school this afternoon. What happened?"

I told him about the skit and Miss Hodge's reaction. "I didn't mean to hurt Miss Eliot's feelings," I added. "I was just trying to be funny."

"You seem to have forgotten what I tried to teach you years ago—about how to treat other people."

"Miss Eliot's classes aren't classes at all. She stammers and stutters around and keeps switching topics. Everyone's always making fun of her. Anyway, I didn't think grown-ups got their feelings hurt the way we do."

"Jessie! You're fifteen years old. Do you really think you and your friends are so different from me and my friends?" Mother asked.

I looked at my mother and had the sensation that I was seeing her for the first time. "Of course you're not different," I said slowly, "just wiser. And I've been stupid and thoughtless. I wish I'd never even thought of putting on a show!"

"It's too late for that kind of wish," said Father. "The question is what are you going to do about it?"

"I don't know what to do. Tell me."

"I don't know either, but I am worried about that woman," said Mother. "She looked so desperate I'm afraid she might do something rash."

"Mother!" She had shocked me. "You mean kill herself?"

"Come now, Laura. It can't have been that bad," Father protested.

"No, I'm sure she's too level-headed to go that far, but I am concerned about her. Neither one of you saw her face."

"I'll go...I'll talk to her. I'll tell her how sorry I am. Will that help do you think?"

"I think it might. Do you know where she lives?"

"Not exactly, but I know she rooms with the organist, Miss Hanford."

"Oh yes, she lives right around the corner from the church. I'll drive you. Will you hitch up Old Nick for me please, Alonzo?"

"I will, but don't you want me to drive her?"

"No, thank you. Perhaps I can be useful. Besides, Johnny should be getting home from the Bennetts' any minute and he'll want to talk to you."

Mother found Miss Hanford's house easily, and we went up the walk together. Miss Hanford answered Mother's knock. She said Miss Eliot had come home at the usual time but had gone straight to her room instead of sharing the customary pot of tea. Miss Hanford led the way upstairs and knocked on Miss Eliot's door. When Miss Eliot said, "Come in," Mother and I breathed sighs of relief.

"I think it will be best if you do this alone," Mother said, "but I'll be downstairs if you need me." I nodded and opened the door.

Not yet dark outside that May evening, it was dark enough in Miss Eliot's room to keep me from seeing her at first. She evidently had a similar problem.

"Who is it?" she asked.

"Jessie Willard. I've come to—"

"No! I don't want to talk. I can't see anyone just now." She came toward me as though she were going to push me out the door. As I stepped back, my heel caught on the sill and I sat down—suddenly and somewhat painfully. Startled and unnerved, I started to cry. Miss Eliot, stunned herself by what she thought she had done, knelt down beside me.

"Oh, Miss Willard! Jessie! Are you all right? Are you hurt? I'm so sorry! I didn't mean to knock you down. Oh please, tell me you're all right!"

"Yes! Yes! I'm quite all right." I put my fingers on her lips. "And you didn't knock me down. I tripped. I came to tell you how sorry I am to have put on that awful skit this afternoon. I was trying to be funny, and of course I greatly exaggerated some of the things that have happened in your classes. I'm afraid I didn't think about how it might affect you. I truly did not set out to hurt your feelings, and if I did, I want you to know how sorry I am. Will you forgive me?"

Miss Eliot stopped dithering and stood up, holding out her hands to help me get up too. She led me to her one comfortable chair and sat herself down on the edge of her bed. She looked at me intently.

"Are you sure you're not hurt?"

"Perfectly sure."

She was silent for a long moment and then spoke with dignity. "When I walked out of the auditorium this afternoon, I thought I would never be able to go back to that school. There was truth in what you said and did in your skit. I am a good teacher for little children. I was successful for years in the primary department of my school in Boston, but when I returned to Chicago to be near my mother, the only position I could find was at Ashby. You have made me see what I was reluctant to acknowledge, that Ashby is not the place for me."

Shaken by the finality of that statement, I started to protest, but Miss Eliot continued. "I will of course go back and finish the year. Now, Miss Hanford and I usually have a cup of afternoon tea. Will you join us?"

While my mother handled that tea party with her customary ease, I was acutely uncomfortable until we were back in the carriage.

My parents decided that I had paid enough of a price for my thought-lessness and that we could put the incident behind us. Miss Hodge still had to be reckoned with, however. When she called me into her office Monday morning, I was still so relieved that Miss Eliot had done nothing rash on Friday, I was not too concerned about the punishment Miss Hodge might impose. It was bad enough, though not for the reason Miss Hodge might have expected. I had to apologize to her and the rest of the school at Tuesday's assembly. I was afraid that Miss Eliot would be further humiliated by hearing the event referred to in public again. I blamed myself for my thoughtless attempt at humor in the skit and said she had been admirably gracious and forgiving about the whole thing.

Miss Eliot finished that year at Ashby amid far less teasing and disruption than she had had before, but she did not return in the fall. I've always thought she showed remarkable courage in going back to the school at all. I learned something from the miserable affair that I unfortunately had not managed to learn from my father.

CHAPTER FIVE

After my morning rest, I feel better, even a little hungry. Nurse Dorothy comes in to check on me. She props me up on two pillows and brings my lunch. I can manage the bread and butter, but I can't cope with the soup without spilling. Dorothy feeds me and talks to me.

"Your son told me you live in Illinois, some town near Chicago?" she says.

I nod.

"My grandparents lived in Chicago when they were first married. They were there at the time of that awful fire, when the city burned up because somebody's cow kicked over a lantern. Were you there then?" she asks.

"I certainly was. I was fifteen, and I actually lived in Chicago with my parents and my brother."

"Were you burned out? My grandparents were. They lost everything. That's why I left Chicago."

"That must have been a terrible experience. It was bad enough for us, and we were among the lucky ones. Our house was spared, but we took in a friend of mine and her family who had gotten out of their house just in time. They lost everything too."

"You must remember all about how it was since you were fifteen."

"I do indeed. I remember how hot it was all that summer of 1871—hot and dry. We had practically no rain. And most of Chicago's buildings were made of wood. The streets were even paved with wooden blocks, and many of the sidewalks were boardwalks. I don't think Mrs. O'Leary's cow had anything to do with it, but the fire apparently did start in her shed. If there hadn't been such a strong wind, the fire might have been checked right there, but the sixty-mile-an-hour gusts spread it too fast and too far for the firemen to have a chance."

Dorothy shook her head in sympathy as I thought back to that terrible October night in 1871. That day my mother and father and Johnny and I had gone to the lake for a picnic lunch because the weather was still so warm. Before we left our house, we could smell the smoke from Saturday night's three-alarm fire that had started in a small woodworking factory and was still smoldering, but we didn't think much about it. Chicago had so many fires in those days. Johnny and I met friends by the lake and had a pleasant afternoon. We went to bed early that night, and I was sound asleep when I heard a pounding on our front door. Hearing Father go downstairs, I went back to sleep. He could take care of whatever was the matter.

Suddenly my shoulder was being shaken.

"Wake up, Jessie. It's me, Maggie Ames. There's a dreadful fire, and we've had to leave our house!" I put on my brace and got dressed as Maggie talked. "Our house wasn't actually burning, but the house next door was, and sparks were already falling on our roof. Father hitched up the horses, and we all crowded into the carriage. Everybody was rushing out of the city. I hope the fire doesn't come as far as your house."

We went downstairs and found the others in the kitchen. Mother was making some hot chocolate and talking to Maggie's sister Kate, who looked stunned. Mrs. Ames was holding Molly, the youngest, who was crying and shivering. The two fathers were out on the front porch, standing on the railing and looking to the north. They came into the kitchen after a few minutes.

"Henry and I are going to try to get to his office," said Father. "He wants to get his files, if he can, and he wants to see what's happened to their house."

"Henry!" Mrs. Ames almost shouted. "You can't go back to that inferno!"

"Don't worry," said Mr. Ames, who was an architect with an office in Courthouse Square. "We'll turn back the minute there's any danger."

The next day we heard all about what they had seen. They had headed north on South Wabash, but when they reached Wabash, they found it jammed with refugees—some in carriages and wagons, most on foot—struggling to hang on to the treasures they had brought from their burning or threatened homes, all hampered in their flight by the treasures abandoned by other people. Pianos, barrels of liquor, toys, birdcages, boxes of china, family portraits—all were being trampled in the rush to escape. Father said it really looked like an inferno as the flames cast a flickering glow over the scene, even though the fire was still several blocks away.

He and Mr. Ames soon gave up trying to buck the fleeing tide and went east to Michigan Avenue. It seemed to have even more wagons than Wabash despite the efforts of the police to block it off, but there was a wide grassy area between the avenue and the railroad tracks that ran along the lake. People had optimistically moved heaps of furniture and other household goods to this area, but Father and Mr. Ames found they could work their way through the piles. They headed west on Washington Street, where the air was still breathable though filled with flying sparks.

When they reached Courthouse Square, the courthouse, the pride of the city, was in flames. The five-and-a-half-ton bell in its tower was still clanging its warning to Chicago. As they watched in dismay, the tower, clock, and bell collapsed and crashed into the fiery basement. Mr. Ames, shielding his face from the heat, dashed across the street to his building, which was just beginning to smoke. He raced up the stairs to his office at the rear of the second floor with Father right behind him. He yanked open his file cupboard and passed papers to Father who stuffed them into two large office wastebaskets. The smoke was much thicker when they left, but they got out before the roof burst into flame.

Clutching the wastebaskets to their chests, they hurried down Clark Street to Van Buren. They were stopped by the heat and the smoke blowing directly at them. They could not distinguish the Ames house, a block away, from its neighbors in the seething wall of flame. Mr. Ames just shook his head. The noise of the wind and the fire made it impossible to make oneself heard. He led the way back up Clark. Father suddenly seized his arm and pointed up the street. In spite of the southwest wind, the fire was now moving south on Clark, directly toward them. They turned east and ran back to Michigan Avenue. Sweating and gasping, they kept going until they reached the railroad tracks by the lake. They felt as though their lungs had been seared. Their coats had a number of small holes where sparks had burned through. Mr. Ames's papers were safe, however, though the top ones were slightly charred in places.

After a brief rest, Father and Mr. Ames headed south again. The chaos on Michigan Avenue was worse than ever, but now at least they were going in the same direction as the refugees. Father led, weaving a path through the heaps of household goods, the slowly moving vehicles—some pulled by men—and the dazed and strangely silent people.

For years I saved the *Chicago Tribune* accounts of that fire. According to those reports, almost one hundred thousand people were left homeless. One of the most frightening aspects of the fire was the speed with which it traveled. After it jumped the Chicago River, it swept eleven blocks to the north in less than an hour, destroying the beautiful homes there as completely as the closely packed cottages of the West Side. Even trees caught fire. The exact number of lives lost was never determined; it was estimated to be between two and three hundred, but only 120 bodies were found. It is amazing that there were so few deaths, considering the scope of the disaster.

The Ames family stayed with us until February 1872, when their new stone house on Van Buren was ready. As an architect, Mr. Ames had more work than he could handle, designing new buildings for the city. His own house was built with such relative speed because he took many of his fees in trade.

Father's office and the large icehouse adjoining it were burned to the ground, but his smaller icehouse was spared. He tacked a temporary office on the front of it and did a small amount of business. There wasn't much ice left because of the heat of the summer. More had been left in the big icehouse, but it had all melted away. Father spent most of his time rebuilding that icehouse so it would be ready when the new ice formed.

For two weeks, Mother and Mrs. Ames, Addie and Janie, and we children provided midday meals for up to fifty refugees. Johnny hauled most of the food in his wagon from the nearest distribution center, on the corner of Wabash and State. Kate and Molly set the table, buffet style, while Maggie and I helped our mothers and Addie and Janie prepare the food. Everybody helped serve and clean up.

All Chicago schools had been closed since the fire, but they were scheduled to reopen on October 23. On the afternoon before the reopening, I suddenly realized that I hadn't seen Maggie for a long time. I looked around outside first, in the yard and on the porch, and then tried the downstairs. Finally I went upstairs to my room—our room—since I had been sharing it with Maggie. She wasn't in sight, but there was a muffled sound from behind my overstuffed chair. I found Maggie crouched on the floor sobbing. I sat down beside her and put my arm around her shoulder, saying nothing. Rigid at first, she finally relaxed and leaned against me. She stopped sobbing, though there were still tears in her eyes.

"I was thinking of my doll," she said at last, "the old one I was given for my first birthday, not the beautiful imported one. Leelee's hair is matted now, and her pink dress is faded and torn, but she's still special, or was. I've lost my house, my own room, my clothes, my books—everything. It seems silly to cry over an old doll, especially when you're fifteen years old, but somehow she—" Maggie stopped.

"I know," I murmured. "Leelee is everything all wrapped up together." I hugged Maggie, and we sat there behind the chair until dark.

CHAPTER SIX

I think of Guy and pray for him every day, of course, but for some reason I have been thinking of him especially this afternoon. Next week he will celebrate his thirtieth birthday—in France. How I wish he were going to be home! How I wish so many things. I know Charlie is proud of his son. I thought Guy had done enough by joining the army and going to Mexico in what his brother Willard calls "that monkey business on the Mexican border." When the First Illinois Artillery, the regiment in which Guy had served as a private, issued its second call for volunteers to be officer candidates, however, Charlie said, "Son, what about this war?" The next day Guy volunteered. It seemed clear from the outset that we would have to get into the war. We couldn't leave it all to the French and English, but I wish Guy hadn't felt obliged to "do his part."

Guy is the handsomest, most charming young man I know—and that is not just a prejudiced mother's view. He can't seem to settle down though: three different colleges before he graduated; a degree in mechanical engineering that he apparently refuses to use; and three different jobs since he graduated, not counting the army. I don't know how many young women he wooed before he decided to marry Mary, and she is certainly not the one I would have chosen for him. We've never had a divorce in the family before, but she is a divorcée. Not only that but she also has a son! Admittedly her first husband walked out on her, but still...I know they will have a hard time socially when Guy comes home. Of course I will try to help them. I'm not at all sure how much I can do, however.

Thinking about Guy's college career makes me think about my own. During my last year at Ashby, I decided that I wanted to go to college. Few young women went in those days, but Mother and Father were supportive of my ambition. I liked learning and was a successful student, winning prizes in French, German, and music when I graduated from Ashby. Maggie Ames planned to go to Pennsylvania College for Women in Pittsburgh, and she and I thought it would be fun if I went there too. That college was spread out over a hilly campus, however, and Mother thought I would have difficulty getting to classes on time. Eventually we heard about Howland College in Union Springs, New York. Founded in 1863, Howland was a small college housed in one building, which had been a large private mansion, made even larger by the addition of Independence Hall in 1865.

One of the charms of the college was its proximity to Cayuga Lake, where the young ladies of Howland skated in the winter. While I couldn't skate, I loved the lake in all seasons. We had a boathouse, and I enjoyed paddling a canoe in the fall before cold weather set in. The winds of upper New York State made spring paddling not only cold but also unsafe.

Howland ranked equally with Wells College in Aurora, New York, about twenty miles away, which was founded at about the same time. I relished my years at Howland and grieved when it closed, not long after I graduated. Most of the girls lived in double rooms on the second floor, but as there were no elevators, I had a small single room on the first floor, opening off the main hall. Surely the best part of my years at Howland was my becoming friends with Ada Eldredge, who has remained my closest friend and who became my sister-in-law in 1891. One of my bridesmaids, Ada met Johnny at the time of my wedding, though they didn't marry for almost ten years. Maggie Ames and I are still good friends—she was my matron of honor—but since she married a University of Pittsburgh man she met at a college dance and settled in Pittsburgh, I seldom see her, though we still exchange letters quite frequently. The Howland girls liked to dance, usually with each other, as there were not many young men around. I used to play the old upright piano in the corner of the living room for them during our free hour after dinner.

Dr. John Porter, Howland's professor of philosophy, sometimes joined me to play his cello. He preferred Bach but was willing to play waltzes for the dancers. His course in early Greek philosophy influenced me more than any other course I've ever taken. I would never have read Plato without his assignments, and I probably would never even have heard of Heraclitus or Parmenides. In the 1870s there were still a good many people who thought women incapable of understanding anything as abstruse as philosophy, but Dr. Porter was obviously not one of them. He seemed to me to be a modern incarnation of Socrates in his approach to teaching. I've always considered myself fortunate to have studied with him.

During my last year at Howland, I received an invitation to visit Alicia Conti Wharton and her family in New Mexico the next summer. When I presented that proposal to my parents, my mother's first reaction was a decided *no*. Even Father, who always wanted me to engage in new ventures, had reservations about this trip. While the nation was at peace, there were several kinds of war being waged in the West. Even in 1876 there were occasional Indian attacks; cattlemen were beginning to come into conflict with sheepmen for fencing off rangeland; and would-be railroad kings were having their own battles. The New Mexicans didn't want a railroad in their territory at all, especially a "damn Yankee" one. Getting to Fort Union to see the Whartons would consequently be a challenge in itself. I could go from Chicago to La Junta, Colorado, by train. It had, in fact, been possible to go clear to the West Coast since 1869, but from La Junta south, travelers had to rely on the stagecoach or some other type of horsepower, and of course "it was a long way for a young lady to travel alone." I got so sick of hearing that!

"I'll be twenty years old by June," I argued. "I have lived away from home for the last three years, except for vacations, and I have traveled from here to upper New York State, which is at least half as far as New Mexico. I really think I can take care of myself, and I really want to go—to see a different part of the country as well as to visit the Whartons. Sooner or later I want to see everything, the whole world!"

When I looked at Mother's face, I realized that I'd better calm down. "I don't want to worry you though," I said slowly. "And you would worry, wouldn't you, every minute until I came back."

"If only someone were going with you, someone we know, I'd worry a good deal less."

"Maybe Ed Wharton knows some officer who will be heading out that way in June," said Father. "I agree with your mother, but I'd be satisfied if you were accompanied by an army officer."

I shook my head doubtfully. "It doesn't seem very likely," I said, "but I'll write to Mrs. Wharton and ask if the colonel knows of any such person."

The colonel did not expect anyone from Chicago, but a young second lieutenant was expected in June, soon after the end of his home leave in St. Louis. The trip to St. Louis was a familiar one to Father, and since that was the obvious route for me to take anyway, Mother and he agreed to let me go.

"I would have preferred to meet him first," Mother said, "but surely we can trust an officer in the United States Army."

"I'm sure we can," said Father, "and I'm even more sure we can trust Jessie's good sense."

They wrote to me at Howland giving their permission for the trip. Like Mother, I wished I could meet Lieutenant Robinson before June. I couldn't help thinking about him, trying to imagine what he was like.

The morning after I got home from Howland, Mother's dressmaker appeared to make me three new dresses: a purple one of cotton faille for traveling, a checked dimity for everyday wear, and a flowered lawn with a matching broad-brimmed hat for special occasions. I was pleased with all of them; I just wished I could do something with my clumpy black boots. Fortunately the stylish long skirts and petticoats covered them quite effectively. The steamer trunk I had shipped home from Howland barely arrived in time to be repacked for New Mexico. For use en route, I had a flowered carpetbag and a hatbox.

Mother, Father, and John, now fifteen and a head taller than I, all drove to the station to see me off. Johnny was going to spend the summer on Uncle Haven's farm, but he looked decidedly wistful.

"I wish I were going with you," he said, not for the first time. "I could carry your bag and just generally make sure you were all right."

"I wish you could come too," I said, "but you'll have a good time on the farm, and I'm sure the lieutenant will take good care of me." I pulled his head down to give him a hug and a kiss.

"Please telegraph us when you arrive," said Father, "and write at least once a week. We don't want your mother worrying any more than she has to."

"No, we certainly don't," I said gravely, but I knew he would worry too if they didn't hear from me regularly.

I hugged them both and boarded the train. Johnny carried my bags onto the Pullman palace car, saw me safely ensconced in my window seat, and thrust a package into my hands as he left. I waved out the window as long as I could see them all and then opened the package. It contained a miniature bowie knife in a leather sheaf with my initials. The enclosed card read, "This is to help you fight off the Indians—and anything else that may threaten you. Love, John."

The trip from Chicago to St. Louis was hot and uneventful. Opening my window certainly allowed for more breeze, but the air was hot and dry and usually smelled of cinders from the engine. The most exciting part of the trip was crossing the Mississippi River on the newly completed Eads Bridge. The river was high, as usual in the spring, and it was truly an impressive sight. As the train pulled into the St. Louis station, I smoothed my hair, which I now wore in a coil around the top of my head, and resecured my hat with hatpins. I speculated once more about Lieutenant Robinson, whom I was about to meet—I hoped. I didn't know what I would do if he didn't meet my train and join me for the rest of the trip. Since there was supposed to be an hour's layover in St. Louis, I left my car and looked eagerly in both directions. A number of people, mostly men, strode purposefully by, but no one in uniform appeared for nearly half an hour. At last I spotted an army cap in the middle of a small crowd of people moving my way. The crowd opened up as it approached, and a young lieutenant emerged with a laughing blond girl clinging to his left arm. Having started forward, I paused and looked questioningly at the young man. He and his companion came to within two paces of me and stopped.

"Are you Miss Willard?" he asked, and when I nodded, he added, "I was sure you must be. Colonel Wharton described you very well. I'm Sam Robinson, and I would like to present my wife, Mrs. Susan Robinson. We were married just last Saturday, and she's going to New Mexico with me. Her family and mine have all come to see us off."

He introduced the members of the two families, giving me a few moments to reassess my position. Miss Hodge would approve, I thought with wry amusement. It's much more seemly to travel with a young man and his wife than with a young man alone—especially such an attractive young man. Oh well, I shrugged philosophically and led the way back to my section of the train.

The Robinsons had the facing seats across the aisle from me. At night the porter transformed the seats into comfortable beds for Susan and me. Sam slept in the upper berth. The newlyweds tried to include me in their conversations, sitting with me from time to time or inviting me to sit with them. We had our meals together in the dining car, but for the first two days I felt like an intruder. Susan seemed so young—young and giggly. She didn't have an idea in her head except Sam. That may be the way brides are supposed to be, I thought, but I couldn't picture myself acting like that under any circumstances. I found myself feeling faintly superior to Susan.

The third morning after breakfast Sam went to smoke a cigar on the observation platform and Susan came to sit beside me.

"May I talk to you?" she asked.

"Of course." I was surprised since we had been talking for two days.

"I mean really talk," said Susan. "I'm so nervous I don't know what to do. You're so calm and sure of yourself, I thought maybe you could help me." She started to bite the edge of her right forefinger.

I closed the book I'd been reading and looked at Susan, noticing for the first time the dark circles under her eyes. I took her hand down from her mouth and held it. "Tell me," I said.

"It's everything all at once," she said, "being married and leaving my family and going so far away. I've never even been on a train before, and I'm afraid of Indians and train robbers and train wrecks and wild animals. And strangers. I don't know a soul in New Mexico. I get so scared at night after Sam leaves that I can't sleep."

"Have you told Sam how scared you are?"

"No. I love him, and I don't want him to think I'm just a baby, to be sorry he married me." Her left forefinger went to her mouth.

"Well, of course you'll have him in New Mexico, and you'll have me for at least two months. I saw Colonel Wharton several times when the Whartons were home on leave last year, and I liked him very much. I know you'll like Mrs. Wharton. She has meant a great deal to me, both as a teacher and as a friend. Have you never been away from home before?"

"Never."

"It's hard the first time," I said, thinking back. "I was miserably homesick when I first went away to school, but that lasted for only about a week. Then I made new friends and was too busy to think about it."

"I don't suppose there will be many women at Fort Union, do you?"

"Probably not, but you'll be busy. You must be excited at the prospect of making your own home.'

Susan brightened. "I am. My mother and my sister and I have been sewing for the last year, making things for my hope chest." I sat back and listened to a description of the embroidered tablecloths, sheets, and pillowcases, as well as the lingerie, that were in that chest.

When Sam came back, Susan greeted him cheerfully and gave my hand a squeeze as she went to sit with him.

That afternoon the train pulled into La Junta, Colorado. Susan and I, surrounded by hand luggage, stood on the station platform while Sam went to the baggage car to make sure the trunks and Susan's hope chest were offloaded. They were to be stored at the station until the weekly freight wagon took them south. We spent the night at the small Spanish-style hotel across the road from the station and set out early the next morning on the stagecoach for Santa Fe.

Drawn by four horses, the coach averaged about two miles an hour, thirty miles a day. Consequently the trip from La Junta to Santa Fe took longer than the trip from St. Louis to La Junta—and was much less comfortable. The coach evidently had no springs, the roads were poor, and the weather was hotter than ever. We kept the window flaps closed to try to keep the dust out, but it crept in through the cracks around the doors and elsewhere in the coach. Even my teeth felt gritty. We spent each day longing for our nightly stop. There was little comfort to be found in the staging posts, but there was enough water to wash our faces and hands as well as to drink, there was a hot meal (hot in both senses as the cooking was Mexican), and there were canvas army cots that we could stretch out on until we started again. When we finally reached Santa Fe, we were still about twenty-four miles from Fort Union, and the only way for us to get there was by army ambulance. In those days, of course, ambulances were horse-drawn too, not like the motor-driven vehicles of today, and they were if anything even less comfortable than the stagecoaches.

When we arrived, exhausted by the days of constant jolting, the heat and dust, the lack of sleep, the poor food, and the lack of sanitary facilities, Susan and I were red-eyed, sunburned, and limp. Sam, who had helped drive the ambulance, had let his beard grow, perforce, and looked like a genuine mountain man.

Just thinking about all this makes me thirsty. I push the button that is supposed to turn on a light and summon a nurse. Perhaps she will bring me some cold lemonade. That's what we had when we finally arrived at the Whartons' house, though it was lukewarm at best. Ice had not yet come to New Mexico. I often thought of Father's largest icehouse while I was there.

Fort Union in the 1860s had replaced Santa Fe as headquarters for the Ninth Military Department, serving as a base for troop movements and becoming an important trade center, which provided supplies to the smaller forts in the surrounding five-hundred-square-mile area. At that time Fort Union was the heart of a bustling town, providing employment to hundreds of harness makers, smiths, carpenters, and wagon builders. There was less activity now than there had been, but the community was much more extensive than I had expected.

When we finally arrived, we were greeted by a reception committee of soldiers and officers, as well as the Wharton family. They knew we were coming by the plume of dust we had raised all the way from Santa Fe. Unlike some forts, Union provided a separate house for each officer and his family. The walls of the buildings were thick, and the roofs overhung to give as much shade as possible. After the formal reception, Martha and Eddy, the Wharton children, led us into their dim and relatively cool living room as everyone talked at once.

After we drank our lemonade, the colonel delegated an aide to show Sam and Susan to their house, and Mrs. Wharton led me down the hall to my room. Four-year-old Martha hung around my doorway as I unpacked but wouldn't come in. When I finished and started back to the living room, however, she took my hand, and when I sat down in a chair covered by an Indian blanket, Martha climbed into my lap.

"You're hard," she said, squirming. "What makes you hard?"

I laughed. "Just one part of me is hard. I have a brace on my right leg."

"Why?"

"Because that leg can't work by itself."

"Can we see it?" asked Eddy, who was seven.

"Leave Miss Willard alone," said his father. "It's not polite to ask such personal questions."

"It's all right," I said. "Of course they're curious." I pulled my skirt above my right knee, carefully keeping the left leg covered, and explained. "The brace keeps the leg stiff so it will bear my weight when I'm walking, but when I want to sit down, I press this little button and it releases the hinge so the brace bends."

"Stand up and show me," said Eddy. "Please," he added, glancing at his father.

I stood up and there was the usual slight click as the brace locked into place.

"May I press this thing?"

I nodded and sat down again as Eddy released the hinge. He beamed in admiration.

"Now," I said, "we'll have to figure out how to make you comfortable, Martha. I can't go through life with an uncomfortable lap. How is it if you sit crosswise, putting your legs over the brace?"

"Better," said Martha, settling back against me.

"Tell me everything that's happening in Chicago," said Mrs. Wharton, coming in from the kitchen. "Did you see my mother before you left?"

"Yes. She came for tea my last day at home." I launched into a description of the major Chicago events since the Whartons' last visit, realizing as I talked that my relationship with Mrs. Wharton had changed from one of teacher and student to one of friends. She evidently recognized the change too and invited me to call her by her first name, making me feel quite grown up.

The nurse, a new one, comes in, having finally noticed my light. She brings me a glass of delicious, freshly squeezed lemonade with plenty of ice. I drink through a bent glass straw and fish some small pieces of ice out of the glass with my fingers. I never really appreciated ice until that trip to New Mexico. Ice was a luxury we took for granted since it was Father's business. The trip taught me a good many things, both about myself and about other people, and I loved almost every minute of it. I doze off again and dream about the Whartons.

CHAPTER SEVEN

During the summer months, New Mexico was so hot that we followed a tropical pattern of life, which I really liked. Reveille sounded at Fort Union at 5:00 a.m. The troops were paraded and the flag was raised at five thirty. Eddy always attended that ceremony, and he invited me to join him. I enjoyed it just as much as he did, and I reveled in the cool early morning air. Next came the daily ride. Martha, who according to her father had been born on a horse, was already at home in a saddle, and Eddy was an accomplished horseman. The colonel was usually too busy to accompany us, but he always insisted on an escort of four soldiers, mounted and armed, in case we were accosted by unfriendly Indians. A few days before we arrived, he had received a dispatch describing a battle at some place in Montana called Little Bighorn. General Custer and a number of his men were killed. Montana was a long way from Fort Union, but there had been rumors of unrest throughout the West though the Indians we saw in La Junta and Santa Fe had seemed peaceful.

About a week after we arrived, I suggested to Alicia that she invite Susan Robinson to join our early rides. Susan looked a bit dubious. "I'd like to come," she said, "but I've never been on a horse. It looks scary—they're so big!"

"We'll find you a small one," said Alicia comfortably, "and we'll start you off in the corral. Remember when you started, Jessie?"

"I'll never forget it. I felt like a queen, the ruler of all I surveyed. I still have a special feeling whenever I'm on a horse."

Susan still looked doubtful, but she agreed to try. She had been somewhat reassured by the extent of the Fort Union community and seemed to have gained some self-confidence since our conversation on the train. After a couple of afternoon lessons in the corral, Alicia thought Susan was ready for the morning ride. She was nervous, but she was determined to keep up. "If Martha can do it, I should be able to," she told me.

Since by seven-thirty the sun was high enough to be blindingly hot, Alicia planned rides that would bring us back to the fort by seven-fifteen. Next came breakfast, prepared by the Mexican cook. Alicia spent three hours each weekday morning at the two-room school for the American, Spanish, and Mexican children of the army and its associated personnel. The legislature had provided for common schools in 1871. A second room had been added to the Union School when Alicia volunteered to teach the younger children.

I wrote letters or wrote in my journal and soon started spending an hour each day reading to Martha and the other four- and five-year-olds. Most schools did not take children so young, but since Alicia thought her daughter would enjoy the experience and might even learn something, she had extended the opportunity to others.

On the way home for lunch one day, Alicia said, "You're good with the children. Have you ever thought of becoming a teacher?"

"Yes, I have. I don't think it's for me though. I've been watching what you do here, and of course I know from personal experience what a good teacher you are, but I don't think I have the patience to be one. Besides, I really don't want to be tied down. I want to be free to travel—to see the whole world!"

Alicia smiled at my enthusiasm. "Life seems to have a way of tying people down, especially women, but I expect you'll manage too see it all somehow."

After lunch there was a long siesta, at least for the women and children, who began to stir after the worst heat of the day was over. Fort Union provided an active social life for its officers, local landowners, and guests from as far away as Las Vegas. Since a number of the officers were unmarried, young single women were particularly welcome. At my first Union ball, I danced almost to the point of exhaustion—flattering no doubt, but not very sensible. I soon discovered that my partners were quite ready to sit out dances and talk, however. Most of them were far from their homes and eager to describe them as well as their families. In addition to balls, there were concerts by the regimental band at the bandstand in the middle of the parade ground, and there were smaller private parties for music or cards. Alicia's mother had managed to send her a piano so she could keep up her playing and teach Martha.

Two weeks after I arrived, the Whartons gave a musical evening in my honor. Alicia and I prepared three piano pieces for four hands, and Edward engaged a Spanish guitar trio from the village below the fort and asked Captain Thomas Wheeler, a baritone, to round out the program. I stood at the door with Alicia to greet and be introduced to the guests. The commander of the fort, General Collins, and his wife; the army surgeon; half a dozen other officers and their wives, including the Robinsons; a dozen civilians; and four young bachelor officers had been invited, and all came.

The big living room, which contained the piano, was lighted by kerosene lamps and half filled with rows of barracks chairs borrowed from the mess hall. Alicia and I started the program with our three duets, concluding with the waltz I wrote for her. Unfamiliar with Spanish music, I especially enjoyed the guitar trio that followed. Tom Wheeler ended the program by singing four songs. After the applause, as people stood up and started to mingle, he approached me.

"You play very well," he said. "You and Mrs. Wharton make a well-matched team. Your little waltz showed that you have a flair for composition as well. Are you still studying music?"

I gave him a long look, but I answered politely, "Thank you. You're so kind. I liked your singing too, especially the Mozart. I did continue studying music at college, but now that I've graduated I'm not sure I'll go on. What about you? Are you still studying?"

Tom laughed. "Where would I find anyone who could teach me anything around here? I've never really felt the need to study, actually. I seem to have a natural gift, and I've never wanted anyone else to spoil it. Where did you go to college? And why? There doesn't seem to be much point in girls getting all that education."

"I went to Howland College in upper New York State. You may be right about the value of my education. You're certainly not alone in your opinion. Both my parents think it's a good idea to develop as many minds as possible—even girls'—and I tend to agree with them. As Jonathan Swift pointed out, since women cannot expect to remain beautiful forever, they do well to cultivate their minds in order to be good companions to their husbands."

"Well, maybe. Who's this fellow Swift?"

"Perhaps an educated wife would be wasted on you. Now if you will excuse me, I must go help Mrs. Wharton serve supper."

I swung off, feeling displeased with Lieutenant Wheeler and not altogether pleased with myself. How did we ever get into that conversation?

I wondered. He's probably not a bad person. I don't suppose he's bright enough to realize that I insulted him anyway. I found Alicia, who stationed me beside the bowl of fruit punch. I served and talked to all the other guests during the evening, forgetting about Tom Wheeler until I got into bed. Then I suddenly heard my father's voice saying that I must learn to think of other people. If I ever saw Tom again, I would try to remember that. But, I thought, he really is an insufferable young man.

Sam and Sue Robinson seemed to have a good time at the musical, though I thought Sue looked rather pale. She was on time for the ride the next morning and thanked Alicia for including her and Sam.

"It was like some of our musical evenings back in St. Louis," she said. "I'm not a bit musical myself, nor is Sam, but we like to listen to people who are. My sister sings in our church choir and sometimes at parties. It was a treat to have something to do last night."

"Are you having trouble finding enough to do?" asked Alicia.

"There isn't much after our morning rides," Sue admitted. "It doesn't take long to tidy up our house, now that we have it arranged as we want it. Of course Sam is gone all day. I sometimes write letters, but it takes so long to get answers that I get discouraged. I'm still homesick, I guess." Her eyes filled.

"We'll have to see if we can't find you some pleasant occupation. The trail is level here. Let's try an easy canter." Alicia signaled the escort, and the four soldiers fanned out protectively.

That night Alicia and I talked about Sue. "She's not interested in helping at the school," I said. "I asked her last week. She said she thought she would enjoy the children, but she doesn't feel qualified to teach—or to do anything else, apparently."

Alicia frowned at me. "She clearly lacks your supreme self-confidence," she said. "Do you suppose she'd like gardening? No, it's just too hot for too much of the year. Sewing? Needlepoint? Rug braiding? Weaving? It would be wonderful to know how to make some of the Indian rugs and blankets."

"Would they share their secrets? I should think they'd want to hoard them."

"I don't know. I am slightly acquainted with one of the weavers in the village. I'll ask her if you think Sue might be interested."

"Maybe we should ask her first. I know she sews. She told me about preparing her trousseau."

The next morning when Alicia proposed the weaving, Sue seemed mildly interested, but she also seemed distracted. She was unlike her usual chatty self during the ride. Halfway home she suddenly slid off her horse and lunged for the side of the trail, retching violently. Alicia handed her rein to me, dismounted, and ran over to Sue. She held Sue's head and patted her back until the episode was over. Then she sent one of the guards to dampen a handkerchief in the nearby brook.

"Better now?" asked Alicia, wiping Sue's forehead.

"Yes, thank you. I'm so embarrassed. There must have been something wrong with the supper I fixed last night, something that disagreed with me."

Alicia regarded her thoughtfully. "Is this the first time you've been sick? Have you been feeling fine every other morning?"

"This is the first time I've actually been sick, but I haven't been feeling very well for the last week or so, especially in the morning. Do you think it's something serious?"

Alicia smiled. "I think it's the only kind of sickness worth having. I think you're going to have a baby."

"Oh! Do you really think so? That would be wonderful! I can't wait to tell Sam. I was afraid I was getting sick, and I was afraid to tell him. But this will make him so happy—and my parents too!"

"Do you feel well enough to ride home, or should we send for a wagon?"

"I feel all right now if you think it's safe to ride."

"We'll go slowly—no trotting or cantering—and this better be your last ride until after the baby is born."

"I'll miss the riding and even more the company. I'll have plenty of sewing and knitting to do now though."

"And of course we'll visit back and forth," I said, smiling. "I'm very happy for you—and Sam too. He'll be so proud."

A few evenings later Tom Wheeler paid a call, ostensibly on the colonel and Alicia. Alicia soon excused herself to put the children to bed, however, and Edward had to finish writing a report. He suggested that Tom and I might encourage him by making some music.

As we were leafing through the sheet music on top of the piano, Tom said, "You don't like me very much, do you."

Surprised that he was sensitive enough to have registered my displeasure, I said, "I hardly know you well enough to have formed an opinion. I will admit, however, that I was put off by your remark about educating girls. We're really not just a subspecies, you know."

"You certainly aren't. I'm not so sure about my two younger sisters and the other girls back in Virginia. They can't seem to talk about anything but beaux and balls."

I looked at him quizzically. "They haven't been to college, have they?"

"No."

"Then don't you see that you're proving my point? If they had been to college, they might talk about other things and you might find them more interesting. But let's drop the subject and give the colonel some music. What would you like to sing?"

Tom chose a collection of Brahms lieder to start with. He really did have a nice voice, I thought, and he was evidently more perceptive than I had given him credit for. He would sing better with some training, however. Too bad he thought he was too good for it.

After Alicia came back and Edward finished his report, all four of us sang, with Alicia and me taking turns at the piano. At the end of the evening, Tom asked if he might come again. As he left Edward said, "Looks as though you've made a conquest, Jess."

"When you're the only apple on the tree, you're bound to look good," I said.

"Oh, come now," said Alicia. "You'd stand out in a whole orchard. But what do you think of Tom?"

"Probably not quite so much as Tom thinks of Tom, but I liked him better tonight than I did the first time I met him. I enjoy 'making music' with him, as Edward calls it."

The next three weeks went by quickly. I saw Tom two or three times a week, either at the Whartons' or at a general social function, and I tried to see Sue at least every other day. She still suffered from morning attacks of nausea, but she was very happy at the prospect of having a baby and kept busy making baby clothes.

The Whartons and I were at dinner one night when we heard a loud knock at the door. Edward answered quickly and found Sam Robinson, looking distraught.

"It's Sue," he said. "She's having terrible cramps, and she's bleeding. I don't know what to do."

Alicia rose from the table. "Jessie and I will come. Just let me ask Rosita to stay with the children. Ed, will you please see if you can find Dr. Reeves?"

"Of course." He patted Sam's shoulder. "Don't worry," he said. "I'll find him and we'll go directly to your house."

He hurried off toward the officers' mess, and Alicia and I ran across the compound to the Robinsons'. We found Sue sitting on the floor with a towel between her legs and with her arms around her knees. She was rocking back and forth and moaning softly. At Alicia's request, Sam picked up Sue and carried her into their bedroom. Assuming the fetal position, Sue reached out for my hand.

"Am I going to lose the baby?" she whispered.

I looked questioningly at Alicia.

"Edward has gone for Dr. Reeves," Alicia said. "He'll save the baby if anyone can. The best thing you can do it try to relax. I'm going to rub your back, and Sam and Jessie will be right here too. Sam, get Jessie a chair, please."

By the time Ed arrived with Dr. Reeves, Sue was feeling better. She was tired and weak, but her cramps had stopped.

"Will the baby be all right now?" she asked.

Dr. Reeves pulled the towel out from between her legs. It was soaked with blood. He took it to the kitchen and dropped it into an empty bucket, and then quietly asked Sam to get a fresh towel.

"I'm afraid you've lost this one," Dr. Reeves told Sue, "but I'm sure there will be others. Now we need to get you to stop bleeding, so I'm going to ask the colonel to order an ambulance and we'll take you to the infirmary."

The Union Infirmary had been created to care for the officers and men stationed at the fort, but it had grown into a small hospital as the community expanded. Sue Robinson spent two weeks there, seriously ill at first but then recovering rapidly. The last few days she spent helping to care for the patients in the children's ward. Having visited her every day, I was surprised to find her there.

"Are you well enough to be up and about so soon?" I asked.

"Oh yes, I'm fine. Still a bit weak but getting stronger all the time." She was holding a small Mexican girl on her lap. "I heard this little one—her name is Juanita—crying and crying yesterday, and there didn't seem to be anyone else around to help her, so I got up and came in. I think she was just lonely and frightened. I can't speak her language, but I'm going to try to learn it. I've been able to do some things for some of the other children too. There just aren't enough nurses here to do all that needs to be done."

"Good for you," I said, feeling a new respect for her. "I'm proud of you."

Sue flushed. "It's about time I stopped brooding about my own troubles. Do you think they would give me a regular job? Accept me as a volunteer, I mean? I don't want to be paid."

"I'm sure they'd be overjoyed to have you. Who's in charge of the children's ward?"

"Sister Maria. Most of the nurses seem to be sisters from the convent in Las Vegas."

"Why don't you talk to her? I shouldn't think you'd have to be a sister to help out. Now I have to get back and start packing. I'll see you tomorrow."

"Packing? You're not leaving yet, are you?" Sue asked in distress.

"No, not for another week, but my trunk is to be picked up by the freight wagon tomorrow. You'll be home before I leave, so it's just goodbye for now."

I could hardly believe that my visit was nearly over. The New Mexico heat had not abated even though it was now September. I would miss all these people, I thought, as I walked into the Whartons' house. I looked forward to being cool again and of course to seeing my own family, but I had certainly had a memorable summer.

The Whartons gave me a going away party on my last Saturday, two days before I was to leave. Mrs. Collins, the commanding general's wife, who had family in New York, had decided to go east with me, to the relief of my parents. The general would provide a strong escort, even though it had turned out that there was no unusual Indian activity in New Mexico that summer.

Shortly before the party Alicia came into my room and sat on my bed for a chat.

"Tom Wheeler will be here tonight, of course," she said. "Ed says Tom has been depressed all week. How do you feel about him now, if you don't mind my asking?"

"No, I don't mind. I have enjoyed making music with him, and for the most part, I have enjoyed his company. But I have no romantic interest in him, if that's what you mean."

"So we'll send you home heart whole?" Alicia smiled as I nodded.

After the musical program and just before supper, Tom asked me to take a walk. The evening was warm, and the stars were bright and close in the clear, dry air. Tom headed for the corral on the far side of the parade ground. He strode along without speaking, then suddenly stopped and looked at me with concern.

"Are you all right?" he asked. "I've been thinking about you so much that I forgot about you. Does that make sense?"

"Not much." I grinned.

"I mean the actual you, the you who has to lug that brace around, who maybe doesn't want to walk all the way to the corral—especially at the pace I was setting. I'm sorry. Shall we stop?"

"No, I can easily go that far, though perhaps a bit more slowly. What have you been thinking about the other me?"

We had reached the corral fence before Tom answered. "I don't want you to go back to Chicago," he said. "I want you to stay here, stay with me...marry me. Will you?"

I put my hand on his arm and looked up at him. "I'm flattered that you should ask me, especially in such a romantic way"—I couldn't help teasing him a little—"but I don't believe you're proposing to that actual me. I think you would like to be married, and I'm the only single white woman available. But I am not ready to be married yet, and even if I were, I could not marry you. We're too different."

"You are certainly different from the girls I knew back home, but I've learned to appreciate that difference. Looking at you, I'm ready to admit that college is a good thing for women. You're special, and I...I've fallen in love with you. I know you're an independent young woman, but I'd like to give you a home and take care of you."

"Independent. That's the key word. I am not ready to give up my independence, for you or anybody else. I do thank you, and I hope you won't be too unhappy with my answer. I'm sure I'll never forget you. Now I think I should get back to the party."

Tom suddenly threw his arms around me and kissed me on the mouth. "That's a good-bye kiss," he said. "I'll walk you back, but I don't want to return to the party."

"Don't bother. I shall be perfectly safe. Good-bye," I said and walked off. Later, when I described the scene to Alicia, she asked what my response to the kiss had been. "Nothing but irritation," I said.

I spent Sunday finishing my packing and making farewell calls. I spent the longest time with the Robinsons and came away feeling satisfied that Sue had found her niche in Fort Union.

Early Monday morning, after many hugs for all the Whartons, especially Martha, I joined Mrs. Collins and we set out for Santa Fe in another army ambulance.

CHAPTER EIGHT

When Nurse Dorothy brings me my breakfast the next day, she also brings a letter from my dear Charlie. Willard sent him a telegram the night of my accident. Poor man, he must have been so worried—and he already has so much to worry him. He is in charge of the Red Cross Convalescent Hospital at the Great Lakes Training Station where the flu epidemic is rampant. He says four thousand of the boys are down with the flu, and there have already been more than twenty-two hundred deaths. He would come to Indianapolis immediately if the situation was not so dire, but obviously he is needed right where he is. His entire building is being used for relatives of the sick. He writes the moving story of the father of one of the boys. After his son died, he asked Charlie if he could stay and help at the hospital. "I have nothing else to do now."

I hope and pray that Charlie doesn't get sick. We have been together so long and have been through so much together that I can't conceive of life without him. We actually met as children. He had to leave school when he was twelve and go to work to help support himself and his younger brother and sister. He got a job as an errand boy, delivering groceries in my neighborhood. He sometimes gave me a ride in his horse-drawn delivery wagon. Although his formal education ended after the eighth grade, he has never stopped educating himself. When we were growing up, most people only went through grammar school. There was in fact only one public high school in the city of Chicago, which then claimed a population of half a million.

Charlie's father, William Henry Bolté, born in Quebec, struggled as a storekeeper to support his wife, Jane Ussher Baker, and their growing family until his lack of success made him decide to move to Chicago. He was a nice man, quiet and soft-spoken, but somehow remote—at least from me. No more successful in Chicago than he had been in Canada, he finally settled on helping his wife run a boarding house.

I really loved Charlie's mother, Jane. Despite the tragedies and disappointments in her life, she was always cheerful, always smiling. Even though she never gave advice, she provided a splendid example for me to follow. It's been five years since she died, and I still miss her. I'm sorry that I never told her what she meant to me. Maybe she knew anyway. She must have known how much she meant to Willard as he was growing up. Having had even less formal education than Charlie, she was much too impressed with my college education, though she spoke as well as I did. So did the rest of her family. She would be pleased that both of our boys have their degrees.

Charlie came back into my life shortly after I came home from New Mexico. Mother, Father, and I had gone to hear General Oliver Otis Howard, the Union general who was appointed commissioner of the Bureau of Refugees, Freedmen, and Abandoned Lands by President Johnson in 1865. An ardent advocate for the education of Negroes, he was largely responsible for the founding of Howard University in Washington. He served as president of the university, which was named for him, from 1869 to 1873 and was now on a speaking tour of the North to raise money for the university. Charlie and his mother had wanted to hear the general too and were sitting in the row behind us. Charlie recognized Mother and Father and spoke to them when the lecture was over.

"Good evening, Mr. and Mrs. Willard," he said. I can still hear him—and still see his handsome, smiling face. "I'm Charlie Bolté. I used to deliver groceries to you years ago. This is my mother, Mrs. Bolté." He turned to me. "You must be little Jessie, only you're not quite so little anymore."

Tall, brown-eyed, black-haired Charlie could make any girl smile. I've never known exactly what he saw in me that made him decide, there and then, that he was going to marry me. I was not a beauty, though my full head of light brown hair, worn up, was satisfactory; my gray-green eyes were said to be interesting; and my smile was said to be friendly. Before we reached the door of the lecture hall, Charlie had asked if he could call on me. A bit surprised, I said yes and agreed that the following Sunday was possible.

He came, and I remember we talked mostly about General Howard's speech. He had told us about the struggles to start schools for the Negroes in the South, about the terrible crimes of the Ku Klux Klan, and about the heroic young men and women who had gone south to teach. The Klan had killed some of them, scared others off, burned schoolhouses, and terrorized Negro teachers and students, but many of the schools survived. Inspired by the courage of those teachers, I thought I might like to become one of them—even though I had told Alicia I didn't want to teach. I sometimes speculate about how different my life would have been if I had done that. Charlie was wise enough not to discourage me or even caution me, but that fall Mother became ill, and I was needed at home.

Charlie courted me for three years, taking me to concerts, plays, and drives in the country and coming to Sunday tea at my house. On a bright October afternoon in 1879, as we were driving along Lake Shore Drive in a hired rig, Charlie guided the horse off the road to a spot that overlooked the lake and stopped.

"Jessie," he said, and I have treasured his words for nearly forty years, "I have admired you ever since I first delivered groceries to your house ten years ago. I first admired your courage and your energy. You weren't going to let a little thing like a crippled leg keep you from what you wanted to do. And that was another thing: you always seemed to know what you wanted. You have a fine mind, Jessie Willard, and you're not afraid to use it. I'm sometimes afraid that I won't be able to keep up with it. I obviously haven't had the education you've had, but I'm working on it. Three years ago, when we met at that lecture, I knew that you were the right woman for me. Every time we have met since then has made me more sure. You're strong and independent, but you're also kind and compassionate. You're beautiful, and I want to spend the rest of my life with you. Will you marry me?"

"That's a lovely speech, Charlie," I said. I looked out at the lake for a long moment. "I think I want to spend the rest of my life with you too. So, yes, I'll marry you."

Charlie took me into his arms and kissed me, and suddenly I felt as though he had released a steel brace that had encased my emotions. As I melted against him, I began to realize for the first time what physical love meant. On the way home, I thought fleetingly of Tom Wheeler and his curiously unstimulating kiss and put my hand through Charlie's arm.

The following Sunday Charlie asked Father for my hand in marriage. Father liked Charlie but was afraid he wouldn't be able to give me the house and carriage and other luxuries I should have. At that time Charlie was a traveling salesman for a thread company earning ten dollars a week plus commissions, and he had almost three hundred dollars in the bank. We thought we could live on that. Father said yes, we could live—in a rented room on beans and coffee. "Not good enough," said Father. Besides, Mother was still ill and relied increasingly on me to run the house. Father concluded by asking us to wait at least a year. That would give Charlie time to build up his income and his savings, and perhaps Mother's health would improve by then.

We waited a good deal longer than a year. Mother and Father finally gave a party announcing our engagement in the spring of 1881. Because Mother suffered severe pains in her chest whenever she exerted herself, I was running the house completely by that time. Addie retired right after the party, comfortably, thanks to Father's generosity. Janie still did the cooking, and Annabel and Richard, the Negro couple who lived in the apartment above the stable, took care of the house, the yard, and the horse.

Mother and I took a drive whenever she felt well enough and the weather was suitable. We visited friends or just enjoyed the country-side or the lake. I had resumed my study of music when I knew I would be home for an extended period and usually played the piano in the eve-ning. Even John seemed to enjoy my playing, on those rare occasions when he was home from the University of Michigan. Two mornings a week I rode one of the Conti horses. Alicia's mother, at seventy-five, still kept four horses and rode nearly every day.

Charlie was on the road during most weeks, but he usually returned to Chicago for weekends. A good salesman and a steady worker, he gradually increased his income and his savings. A wonderfully patient man, he lost his temper only once in those years of waiting. The result was a memorable quarrel. He and I were sitting on our front porch one Saturday evening in 1882. Charlie had sat up on a train most of Friday night to get home for the weekend and had spent the next day in the main office. He was tired and hot.

"This is no way to live, Jessie," he said. "I want you, all of you, and all to myself. I want to come home to our house, not your parents'—or my parents' either, though we don't see much of them. I guess you think you're too good for the Boltés."

"Charlie! You know that's not true. I don't know your father very well, but I think your mother is wonderful, and I have every intention of marrying you as soon as—"

"Oh sure, as soon as it's convenient for everybody else. What about me? I've been waiting and slaving for you for nearly six years. We announced our engagement almost two years ago, but we're no closer than we ever were to getting married. I'm human, you know, and all this hanging around is wearing me down."

"Nobody is making you hang around. I'm human too, and I'm not any happier than you are. I didn't plan things this way, but I can't just go off and leave my mother. She needs me."

"And of course she comes first. And then your father, and then your brother, and then God knows who. You're the most important person in my life, and as your prospective husband, I'm supposed to be the most important in yours. Instead I'll just have to get in line until the others die off and then maybe you'll marry me."

"Charlie! Don't say such things! If you're in such a hurry, go find yourself a girl with no responsibilities!"

"Maybe I will." Charlie took the porch steps in one stride and stalked angrily down South Wabash.

I couldn't believe we had let the quarrel go so far so fast. I couldn't believe Charlie was really gone. For once in my life, I simply didn't know what to do. And then I heard Mother's soft voice. I had not realized that she and Father were sitting in the living room right by the window opening onto the porch. They had heard everything Charlie and I said. To avoid hearing their reaction, I moved around to the side porch. I spent an unhappy hour there, torn between anger and dismay, until I heard Charlie's footsteps coming up the walk.

He apologized for some of the things he had said, but he made it clear that his basic position was unchanged. I was just starting to say how sorry I was when Father called us into the living room.

"Your mother and I have a proposal to make," he said. "We know that you are eager to be married, but Jessie has made herself so indispensable in this house I don't see how we can let her go. Her bedroom is big enough for two people, and the house if big enough so we wouldn't constantly be on top of one another. You could go on saving your money, Charlie, and we'd still have Jessie's help. What do you think? I know you want your own home, but could you be happy if you got married and lived here, at least for a time?"

Saying nothing, I turned to Charlie. I knew him well enough that it would be a mistake to push him, though I couldn't help smiling. Eventually he smiled too. "Shall we get married, Miss Jessie?" he said.

We chose December 18 because Charlie had a year-end vacation coming. The three ushers for the wedding were Charlie's brothers, Philip and Anson, and my brother, John, and the three bridesmaids included Ada Eldredge and Grace Baker, who had attended Howland with me. The matron of honor was my old friend Maggie Ames, now North; she had married Robert North three years earlier. The best man was Jack Mason, who worked with Charlie for the Thurston Thread Company. Our minister suggested that I might like to enter from the side door near the altar, but I chose to walk down the long aisle on Father's arm.

Mother and I wanted the reception at our house, and Father agreed, but reluctantly, because he was afraid Mother would overexert herself. When he stipulated that the affair should be catered, Janie was so upset that she threatened to quit unless she was permitted to do the party for "Little Jessie." Richard and Annabel were quite ready to help, and Addie came out of retirement to lend a hand. We all agreed that the wedding cake should be her raisin-nut specialty.

I wore Mother's wedding gown, though it had to be made over because I was so much shorter than she. The bridesmaids wore dark red velvet dresses, the same shade as the roses in the red and white bouquets that decorated the church and the house. Charlie and the other men in the wedding party wore the conventional morning coats and striped trousers.

While Charlie and I were upstairs changing to traveling clothes, John finally managed to have a conversation with Ada Eldredge. He told me later that he had been admiring her ever since she arrived from Union Spring three days earlier. He had met her when he attended my graduation from Howland, but he had been too young then to pay attention to other graduating seniors. Now that he was a college graduate himself and held a responsible position in Father's ice company, the difference in ages seemed to John to have vanished. It evidently didn't bother Ada either. The two were engrossed in each other when Charlie and I came downstairs. The next wedding in the family, some years later, was in fact John and Ada's.

We hugged and kissed both pairs of parents, waved to everyone else, and set off by carriage for Chicago's Union Station. Father had given us a trip to New York as a wedding present. We had a stateroom so we could have some time completely to ourselves. We were both so nervous when we reached the stateroom, however, that we weren't at all sure we wanted to be alone.

"Would you like to go to the dining car and get something to eat?" Charlie asked. He hung up his coat and put his new silk hat on the shelf in the tiny closet.

"I'm not very hungry," I said, thinking of all the food at the reception, "but I would like a cup of coffee."

"Good." We smiled at each other in relief and started down the Pullman aisle with me in front, Charlie's hand on my arm to steady me. He was somewhat hampered by the bustle on my green faille going-away dress, but the diner was only two cars away.

I had been to New York City a number of times. Father had taken me there to see an orthopedic specialist when I was five, before I got my first brace, and I had sometimes stayed in the city with friends on the way to or from Howland. Charlie, who had never been there before, was eagerly looking forward to the sights. Perhaps to show himself as a man of the world in the diner, he decided we should have wine rather than coffee. In the warm glow of the gas lamps, we toasted each other as the train chugged through the cold winter night.

Back in the stateroom, our nervousness disappeared. Charlie helped me take off my dress and gently removed my brace after I showed him how. Despite the reassurance of my doctor, I was still afraid that I might not be a satisfactory sexual partner for Charlie. Our first attempt was somewhat painful for me, but he was satisfied, and I loved feeling the naked Charlie against my naked self. He was so considerate that within a few nights he satisfied me too.

After Charlie signed the register at the Windsor Hotel on Fifth Avenue, a bellboy picked up our bags and escorted us to the elevator and then to our room on the fourth floor. The high-ceilinged room, which had windows facing west, contained a large double bed with a carved mahogany headboard, two heavy mahogany bureaus with mirrors, a small horsehair sofa, two upholstered chairs with antimacassars, and a round mahogany table between the chairs. Looking out the window I could see the Hudson River, gleaming silver in the winter sunlight. Traffic on the river consisted largely of steamships, but the numerous masts showed that many vessels were still sail powered. The traffic on Fifth Avenue consisted of shiny carriages, buses, drays, and occasional moving vans—all horse drawn. Like Chicago's streets, many of New York's were paved with wooden blocks, though some had been paved with granite blocks quarried in Connecticut. As dusk closed in, a lamplighter lit the avenue's gas lamps, and Charlie lit the two lamps on the wall of our room and the candelabrum on the table.

On our second night, we went to hear *Orfeo*, with Adeline Patti singing Eurydice. Charlie was beginning to like classical music, though he was still not quite sure about opera. He was more enthusiastic about the performance of *Hamlet* with Edwin Booth, which we saw two nights later. For several years after his brother, John Wilkes Booth, had shot President Lincoln, Edwin had abandoned his career, but critics found him better than ever when he returned to the stage.

During the day Charlie and I toured the city, usually traveling on one of the buses with its wooden benches along each side. The straw on the floor was never enough to keep my feet warm. Sometimes we went by El, the elevated train that was New York's equivalent of the trolley. Just north of Central Park there were many small farms. It was too cold for anything to be growing in the fields, but the goats, sheep, chickens, and geese enlivened the scene. The cold snap lasted long enough to freeze the pond in the park. When we passed the flag flying, meaning the ice was safe for skating, Charlie suggested we try it.

"You go," I said. "I've never been able to manage skates. In fact, I'm really afraid of ice. I'll be perfectly happy back at the hotel. I should write some letters anyway, and I'll enjoy thinking of you skating."

"Let's get off. I have an idea," said Charlie. We got off the bus and Charlie said, "Wait here." He walked to a large shed near the bonfire by the pond and soon came back, smiling broadly.

"They have skates to rent and a chair with runners. It will be almost like skating for you, but you won't have to do any work."

Charlie and the proprietor of the shed got me settled and tucked in with a heavy wool carriage robe. Then Charlie strapped on his skates, which were single blades attached to wooden platforms, and off we went. Many other people of all ages were enjoying the ice: children with red and blue and green and white striped scarves, frequently falling down and picking themselves up again; men with derby hats, skating alone; and couples, men, and women skating with their hands crossed. Most of the women, like me, wore fur hats and long coats with fur collars. I also had a fur muff. On the bank near the shed stood a man with an organ grinder grinding out "Hail, Hail, the Gang's All Here." Charlie was a good skater, and the chair moved easily on the ice. No longer afraid, I laughed with pleasure as he spun me around when we reached the end of the pond.

The next day we took a bus downtown to visit Trinity Church. The avenue was lined with telegraph poles with as many as fourteen crossarms. Along the street, vendors peddled dried ferns, grease erasers to remove spots, needle threaders, and boutonnieres of artificial flowers, all selling for ten cents. The chief attraction of Trinity was its tower, which rose two hundred and eighty-four feet, making its peak the highest in New York. It was a struggle for me to climb the steps, but the view of the city, the rivers, the bay, and the stone towers of the still unfinished Brooklyn Bridge was ample reward.

Another day we went to Madison Square to see a most extraordinary sight: the torch-bearing arm of the Statue of Liberty. Sent over from France for the Philadelphia Centennial Exposition, it had been brought to New York to await the decisions about where in the harbor to put the statue and how to pay for its erection. Charlie eagerly climbed the steps to the railed platform just below the torch's flame, but still recovering from the Trinity climb, I was content to admire the enormous copper arm from below.

On Christmas Eve and throughout Christmas morning it snowed. We had planned to go to church but were deterred by the near-blizzard conditions. We spent most of the day in our room, talking and packing in preparation for our departure the next afternoon. We had a splendid Christmas dinner in the hotel dining room, and when we finished, the snow had stopped and the wind had died down. Charlie had a quiet conversation with the desk clerk on our way to the elevator. At five o'clock he jumped to his feet.

"Come on, Jess," he said. "Put on your coat and everything else you need to keep warm. We're going out."

"Where on earth can we go in all this snow?"

"You'll see. Come on, we need some fresh air."

We bundled up, went down in the elevator, and walked out the front door of the hotel. At the curb stood an open sleigh with a matched pair of black horses and a coachman wearing a top hat and a long black-and-white-striped scarf. He grinned at us and tipped his hat as the hotel doorman opened the door of the sleigh and helped us arrange the buffalo robe over our laps. The coachman took us to Central Park, where everyone else in New York had apparently decided to go that Christmas night. Most of the horses wore silver harness bells. Their hoofbeats were muffled, and the runners made a hissing sound in the snow. Many of the sleighs had brightly enameled sides of green, maroon, or black, and some had winter scenes painted on their doors, which became visible as the nearly full moon broke through the clouds.

"What a lovely idea, Charlie," I said as we returned to our hotel. "This is a perfect way to end our trip. Thank you for the happiest Christmas I've ever had."

Charlie put his arm around my shoulders and hugged me. "It's the happiest I've ever had too," he said.

The next day we boarded the train for Chicago.

CHAPTER NINE

D r. MacCracken comes to visit me in the afternoon. He apparently took care of me the night I arrived at the hospital. I didn't remember anything about that, but I remembered him from the last time I broke my leg. A normally cheerful man, he is scowling today.

"What are we going to do with your son?" he asks. "He should know better than to have his floor waxed just when you're coming for a visit!"

"He didn't know I was coming until the last minute, so don't be too hard on the poor boy."

"Hmmph." The doctor sits on the edge of my bed and takes my hand. He looks carefully at my eyes. "How's the head?" he asks. "Does it still ache?"

"Hardly at all."

"Good. We'll let you sit up for supper—in your bed, of course. Makes it easier to eat. Where's your husband? I remember him from last time."

I show him part of Charlie's letter, and he shakes his head sadly.

"That wretched influenza is everywhere. You see you don't get it, hear? We can fix a broken leg easily, but flu is another matter." He pats my hand and leaves.

I have always had good doctors, both capable and concerned. I think back to Dr. Crandall, who took care of me during my first pregnancy. I never had an easy pregnancy, but the first one was the worst. My morning sickness lasted most of the day for more than five months. Fortunately Mother's condition eased during that year so she was able to resume many of the household chores.

"This is not the way it's supposed to be, though!" I said ruefully as Mother poured me a cup of afternoon tea.

"Never you mind," said Mother. "I think the idea of having a grandchild has wrought a miraculous cure for me, so don't you fret. Will you eat some cinnamon toast?"

"Yes, please. I feel a little hungry."

"At last! I wish you could manage to eat more. I'm sure that baby needs more nourishment, to say nothing of you." She studied me for a moment. "You really don't look very well. Let's see if we can't build you up a bit before Charlie comes home." Charlie, who still spent most of each week on the road, was on an extended trip, as the Thurston Thread Company was trying to expand its sales into the neighboring states.

"I do try to eat," I said, "but even if I succeed, it doesn't stay down."

As the spring progressed I felt better, however, and began to gain some weight. Charlie shared my excitement over the baby's kicks and spent several weekends converting the bedroom next to ours into a nursery, painting and building shelves. I sat in a rocker in the middle of the room, watching Charlie and knitting booties and soakers to be worn over diapers.

"What shall we call it if it's a boy?" asked Charlie.

"Why, Charles Guy, of course. I think it is a boy, but suppose it's a girl. What could we call her?"

"Why, Jessie Willard, of course." Charlie grinned.

The summer of 1883 was another hot one and, I thought, a particularly long one. The baby was due the first week of September. I developed a severe backache on August 29th and went into labor that night. Charlie was on the road, but when the pains became so acute I couldn't help crying out, I was glad he wasn't with me. Like most of my friends, I had decided to have the baby at home. As soon as Mother was sure the labor had really started, she sent Father for the doctor, a young man by the name of Martin Crandall, who had taken over the practice of Dr. Adams when he retired.

When Dr. Crandall arrived, I was lying on my back clinging with both hands to the crossbar of the spool bed above my head. Mother stood by the bed and every few minutes wiped my face with a damp washcloth.

"I can't stand much more of this, Dr. Crandall," I whispered.

"Let's see how you're doing," he said. "If you're far enough along, we'll put you to sleep." After a careful examination, he straightened up. "I think we can safely give you a dose of chloroform now," he said briskly, opening his black bag.

The baby came soon, but Mother barely had time to name him, to call him Charles Guy, before he died.

When I wakened, I smiled and held out my arms. "Is it a Charlie or a Jessie?" I said.

The Thurston Company managed to track Charlie down the next morning, and he came home that afternoon. I had kept my composure until he sat down on the bed and took me into his arms. Then I broke down.

"It's all my fault," I sobbed. "I knew I never could have children. There's something terribly wrong with me—and you never should have married me!"

Charlie just held me tighter until my sobs gradually ceased. "The first and most important thing, to me, is that you're all right," he said. "There's nothing the matter with you. Dr. Crandall doesn't know exactly what went wrong with the baby, but he's certain that you will have more children who will be perfectly healthy. He says these things just happen sometimes. You simply must not blame yourself. Will you promise you won't?"

"I'll try not to," I said, but I resolved to have my own conversation with Dr. Crandall. When I talked to him a few days later, he repeated what he had told Charlie.

I've never forgotten my disappointment over the loss of that first child, but within four months I was pregnant again. John Willard Bolté was born on September 1, 1884, in the middle of another heat wave. A somewhat small baby, he was healthy and active. As the first grandchild for both the Boltés and Willards, he would surely have been spoiled if it hadn't been for me. I had to be the disciplinarian since Charlie was away so much. Grandfather Alonzo spent a good deal of time with Will, as he called his grandson, taking him for rides in the surrey as soon as he was old enough to sit on the seat. The horse was an old plug named Frank. Father had to keep jerking on the reins to prevent Frank from slowing down to a walk, but at least once on each trip old Frank would suddenly stretch his neck forward to get some slack in the reins, kick the dashboard with both hind feet, and start to run. Willard understandably became afraid of horses. The day the neighbors' dog went mad in the backyard next door and raced around in foaming circles until a policeman came and shot him with a revolver made Willard afraid of both dogs and revolvers.

When Willard was three and a half, Guy Willard was born. I never wanted to hyphenate my maiden name with Bolté, but I did want the name to be preserved by all my children—except poor little Charles Guy. Having a baby brother gave Will a keen sense of responsibility and made him suppress his own fears as he sought to protect Guy. Whether thanks to Will's care or to his own personality, Guy never shared Will's fears.

Soon after the birth of our second son, it occurred to me that it might be time for Charlie to find a new job, one that would give him a greater prospect for advancement and that would not require so much traveling. I broached the subject one Sunday afternoon when the little boys and their grandparents were all napping.

Having made the suggestion, I said, "It would be nice for all of us, but especially for me, to have you here during the week."

Charlie smiled. "Of course I'd like that too. I'm doing pretty well with Thurston though, increasing my sales and making more money each year."

"I suppose that's part of the trouble. You're such a good salesman that they'll never take you off the road, never give you a management position."

Charlie shrugged. "I like what I'm doing well enough, except that it keeps me away so much. I don't especially want to be part of the management."

"Don't you have any ambition?"

"I want to be able to provide a comfortable, happy life for you and the children," he said thoughtfully. "I don't want to be president of the United States—or of anything else, if that's what you mean."

"No, but wouldn't you like to have your own business instead of always working for someone else?"

"Maybe someday. I'm not in a hurry to make a change, though."

I was silent, but I had just begun my campaign. I returned to it from time to time during the next six months until Charlie finally began to look around.

"I have good news," he said one Saturday afternoon when he came home later than usual. "At least I hope you'll think it's good."

I smiled expectantly.

"I've seen Sam Harmon three times in the last several weeks. He's the president of Harmony Silks, and today he offered me a job. He wants me to be vice president in charge of sales."

"Charlie! That's wonderful! Does that mean you won't have to travel any more?"

"Not quite, but I'll be on the road much less. Mostly I'll be telling other people where to go and what to do. And it will mean more money."

I put my arms around his neck and gave him a big hug. "That is good news indeed," I said, "and it's well timed, because were going to have another baby."

Charlie returned the hug. "Maybe the time has come for us to get our own home. I don't think we should go on living here with three young children. Do you?"

"No. I think Mother needs peace and quiet more than anything I might still be able to do for her."

Mother and Father reluctantly agreed that it was time for us to establish a separate household.

"I'll miss you," said Mother, who was as usual resting on the living room couch. "But at least you won't be moving far away. You won't, will you?"

"Oh no," said Charlie. "We'll stay right in Chicago. The Harmony office is just two blocks from Alonzo's."

Father was bouncing five-year-old Willard on one knee and one-and-a-half-year-old Guy on the other. Guy's laughter made all the rest of us smile.

"Of course I won't miss these fellows a bit," said Father. "Still, I suppose they might come and see us once in a while. Do you suppose you might, Will? Come and bring Guy?" Will nodded solemnly and leaned back against his grandfather.

We moved into 3131 Graves Place in November 1889, in time to celebrate Thanksgiving—Lincoln had revived the custom in 1863—with a feast prepared by Lucy Lee and me. Lucy Lee, the daughter of a friend of Janie, was our young black maid. I felt quite well throughout my fourth pregnancy, but as it progressed I relied more and more on Lucy for lifting and carrying as well as doing the laundry. Lucy soon became as indispensable to us as Janie was to my parents.

Linda Willard Bolté was born on March 2, 1890, the Willards' first and only granddaughter until Johnny's daughter Margaret was born exactly two years later. Charlie loved his little boys, but he was enchanted by his little girl, as was Mother. They often sat and watched the baby together, exclaiming over each new move she made.

Never totally satisfied with the Graves Place house and quite dissatisfied after Linda's birth, I decided we must move again. I found a larger and generally more suitable house on Forest Avenue. Six weeks before the move, Charlie came down with typhoid fever. His temperature was so high that Dr. Crandall prescribed ice packs for his abdomen as well as his head, but for once my mild-mannered husband rebelled. Every time I tried to apply a cooling pack, he would seize it and hurl it across the room. The best I could do was wipe his face and arms and hands with damp cloths cooled by the rejected ice. Charlie lost a lot of weight, and as moving day approached, he was still too weak to walk though the fever was down. There was not an ambulance to be had in the whole city of Chicago, and I didn't know what I was going to do until Joe Bates came to visit Charlie.

When he was twenty-one, Charlie had joined the First Illinois Infantry of the National Guard, and by this time he was a captain. Joe Bates, who had served with him for twelve years, said he thought the First had enough political influence to secure a police patrol wagon in which to move Charlie. Joe was successful, and on moving day the patrol wagon backed up to the door while the neighbors gathered to see who was going to be arrested. Two large policemen carried Charlie downstairs on a stretcher.

"What's the matter with the poor felly?" the Irish sergeant asked.

"He's had a bout of typhoid fever," I said, "but he's—"

"What! Here, Mike, put him down. We can't take him in the wagon. Typhoid's ketchin'!"

"Put him down where?" said Mike. "There's nothing left to put him on." All the furniture had been moved out that morning. Charlie had sat on the last box of clothing to wait for the police.

"Stop!" I said. "Don't you dare put him down! As I started to tell you, he's completely cured of the typhoid. He's not sick at all anymore; he's just very weak."

"Sorry, lady, rules is rules."

"Sergeant, do you seriously mean to tell me that there is a police regulation forbidding you to help an officer of the Illinois National Guard who badly needs help?"

Stubborn silence came from the sergeant.

"I will personally disinfect your wagon after you get him to Forest Avenue. Will that make you feel better?"

Eight-month-old Linda, who was in my arms, began to cry, setting off two-and-a-half-year-old Guy, who was clinging to my skirt.

"Aw, come on, Sarge," said Mike. "These folks need help. The felly won't be in the wagon for more than about twenty minutes. I'll wash it out myself when we get back."

The sergeant grunted in disgust, but he started for the door, surprising Mike into a lurch that nearly sent Charlie cascading to the floor. "Sorry," said Mike, quickly righting the stretcher. "I've got you now though, and you'll soon be in your new house." Charlie started coughing to give vent to the laughter he had been suppressing.

Father and Richard drove up in the family carriage as Charlie was being installed in the police wagon. I handed Linda to her grandfather while Richard helped the boys into the carriage and gathered up the last suitcases. At the new house, Lucy Lee, Annabel, and Richard helped me unpack the kitchenware and china, lay the rugs, and make the beds. Finally Richard carried Charlie, who had been lying on the porch swing, upstairs to his own bed. The new house evidently agreed with Charlie, as he quickly began to regain his strength and returned to work in a couple of weeks.

CHAPTER TEN

In the afternoon Willard, Jess, and the three boys come to see me. I must say they are an attractive, cheery lot—and Jess must have threatened the boys with dire consequences if they didn't behave. They behave beautifully and are properly admired by Dr. MacCracken and Nurse Dorothy, who also come to see me. Thank goodness the doctor doesn't scold Willard and Jess for their slippery floor. They feel guilty enough as it is. The doctor decides I am well enough to be put into a wheelchair and given a change of scene. Willard and Dr. MacCracken lift me into the chair, which has a kind of shelf for my left leg, and the boys start to quarrel over which one will push me. Jess instantly settles it by appointing John, the oldest and tallest. Eleven now, he is already as tall as I am. He carefully pushes me out of my room and down the corridor to the solarium, a bright and sunny room with enough chairs for everyone to sit down. It also has a box full of blocks in one corner so the boys have something to entertain them while the rest of us talk.

Willard has received a letter from Guy that contains encouraging news about the war. Our boys have been moving in what he calls "the biggest advance since the Somme of 1916, I believe," putting the Boches in "an extremely precarious position." He describes a letter found on a German prisoner from his father, saying "If you come across the accursed Yankees, retreat or surrender, for they will do neither." Guy's letter continued, "Son took the advice of Vater and did the latter, as his officers have a pleasant habit of putting a machine gun behind their men to see that they keep going in the right direction." There is no question of the veracity of this.

"Everybody is here—Italians, Tommies, French, and ourselves, each to their specialty. The Italians have done fairly well in one sector, but mostly they build roads and bury the dead. The British handle their tanks and get sixty percent of the credit for the truly splendid control of the air. The Yanks are mostly used as attack troops (and they are whales at it), and the French form the solid, comforting backbone of the whole works—the wonder and admiration of all who come in contact with them."

This is all very encouraging, but in his next paragraph he describes how close he came to being blown to pieces. He was having a hard time controlling his new horse, an eighteen-hand mare named Agnes who was apparently determined to dislodge her rider. Suddenly she stopped bucking and started galloping up the country lane. "She was obviously racing the only Boche plane I saw all day that was coming up behind us," he writes. "Then almost without pausing she leaped over the hedge on the left-hand side of the road and charged across the wheat field. Behind us I heard four small bombs neatly dropped in the road we had just left. Agnes got an extra helping of oats that night."

"It's a good thing Guy finally learned to manage a horse," I say as I finish his letter. During his first few weeks at the French artillery training camp at Saumur, he had spent much of his time learning to ride and care for a horse.

"He always was a lucky so-and-so," says Willard. "You don't need to worry about him. His luck is sure to bring him home safely."

"Knock wood when you say that, will you please?" Jess says, and I nod in agreement. We are not generally superstitious, but we don't believe in tempting fate. She's too fickle.

I look at Willard's boys and hope and pray they will never have to fight a war. I am struck, as I have been before, with how much Charles

Guy II, his youngest, looks like Alonzo Willard Bolté, my youngest. Charles Guy is seven now. He has already lived two years longer than my Alonzo, whom we always called Donny to distinguish him from his grandfather. I find I am tired and ask to be taken back to my room. The boys all kiss me gently and promise to come again soon.

Lying in my bed again, I continue to think about Donny. Father was really pleased to have a grandson named for him. Born just after Mother died, the baby was a comfort to all of us. On Christmas night, 1892, after we had all spent a happy day together, Mother collapsed as she was getting ready for bed. Dr. Crandall, who attended her, held out little hope. Mother could still speak, but she was partially paralyzed. I spent each afternoon with her, holding her hand and talking about the children mostly, though she was also interested in hearing about Jane Addams, whom I had recently heard speak. Addams was the founder of Hull House, a social settlement in downtown Chicago, and Mother and I both admired her for what she was trying to do.

Mother lingered into February, slipped into a coma the night of the third, and died early the next morning. Father was with her, but I was not, to my sorrow. She was seventy-five. Trite as it sounds, I felt as though I had lost my best friend. Father bore up well until after the funeral when I saw him cry for the first time in my life. We had been helping to take the remains of the funeral baked meats to the kitchen, where the sight of Janie in tears made us both break down. We all wept together.

Twelve days after Mother died, Alonzo Willard Bolté was born. He entranced Father, partly because of his name but also because of his sunny disposition. That spring I decided we needed a bigger house and found one in Winnetka, a small town seventeen miles north of Chicago, still on Lake Michigan. When Father sold his big house, Charlie and I invited him to live with us. We would have plenty of room in the new place, which we were renting for seventy dollars a month. That was high for the time and place, but the house had a porch that ran around three sides; three living rooms; eight bedrooms, not counting those on the third floor; and a cupola on top of the roof. Not surprisingly, in view of the fourteen-foot ceilings, the furnace ate forty tons of anthracite a year to keep the house a few degrees above freezing—except in the coldest weather. The barn, heated by the cow and the three horses, was somewhat warmer.

Charlie's father, William Henry Bolté, had died in 1884. His wife continued to run the boarding house, but now, well into her sixties, she was beginning to feel somewhat hampered by her arthritis.

"Jessie, what would you think of having Mother live with us in the new house?" Charlie asked shortly after we moved.

"Oh! Would she come? I'd be happy to have her, and we certainly have enough room. I'm sure you'll worry about her much less if she's with us, and so will I."

Jane Bolté accepted our offer with pleasure. Her only concern was for her boarders, but she managed to sell her house to a young couple who were willing to keep them on.

Our new household thus included Charlie and me, four children, two grandparents, and one servant. Annabel and Richard, who had worked for my parents for years, did not want to live so far out in the country and declined our offer of employment. Since it was clearly unreasonable to expect Lucy Lee to do all the work for such a large house and so many people, I hired a cousin of Lucy's named Kate. Grandfather Alonzo, now seventy-six, had retired, but he was still very active and enjoyed driving Jane and the children wherever they wanted to go. I preferred to drive myself. A hired man took care of the cow and horses, the lawn, the garden, and the furnace for twenty-five dollars a month. He slept in the basement in winter, the barn in summer.

Winnetka in 1893 consisted of about twelve hundred people. It was bounded on the east by Lake Michigan, with bluffs as high as eighty feet at the north end, and on the west by Skokie Swamp, a haven for crawfish and bullheads and violets and bob-o-links and meadowlarks and small boys. Some misguided speculator had plotted a portion of the swamp and laid two miles of wooden sidewalks along his phantom streets. When the water was high, Willard and Guy and their friends used to break off a fifteen-foot section of sidewalk and use it for a raft. Winnetka had similar sidewalks and streets surfaced with nothing but Cook County clay, meaning mud in the spring and dust in the summer. The streets were lighted with kerosene lamps on each corner. The town had one telephone, in Mrs. Willy's candy store, and it cost a quarter to call Chicago. The butcher's boy and the grocer's boy came to the back door each morning to take the day's orders and delivered them in the afternoon The food bill for the household of eleven sometimes ran as high as fifty dollars a month because I liked to set a good table, including turkey or great rolled roasts of beef for Sunday dinner. Since Charlie's salary had increased to $5,000 a year, we were not worried about money. Busy with the family and managing the household, I was content. Occasionally I took the train into Chicago to hear a lecture or to have dinner and attend a concert with Charlie. I still played the piano and rode my horse two or three times a week.

The serenity of the family was shattered in the spring of 1898. A family friend had recently given Willard a small rifle, and like a fool I had overcome my fear of firearms and allowed him to keep it. The third weekend in May, a young man named Cal Williams, the grandson of an old friend of Father's, came to visit us. On Saturday morning, Willard led his sister Linda, Cal, and a whole troop of younger children on a walk up Sheridan Road into Hubbard's Woods. The youngest was Donny. He trailed along behind carrying a huge branch and complaining because the others walked too fast for his short legs. He made it home with his branch, however. After lunch Cal agreed to show Willard how to shoot his rifle. Cal fastened a paper target to the wall of a small shed adjacent to the barn, and after some instruction, he and Willard too turns shooting while the younger children watched. After a few rounds, they decided to see if the bullets were going through the wall. Everyone went in to look. The bullets were going through not just one but both walls. The troop went back out, and Cal and Willard started shooting again. Then they noticed Donny was missing.

"Maybe he went back to the house," said Cal.

"I'll go see," said Linda, and she ran off.

"Maybe he's in the barn. I'll look," said Guy.

Willard hesitated a moment but then started walking toward the shed.

"He can't be in there," muttered Cal.

But he was, lying on his back with a bullet hole in the middle of his forehead. He was still alive. We learned all these details later when Cal told us all about it. We knew nothing until Cal ran up onto the porch, threw open the front door, and shouted, "There's been an accident!'

Charlie and I rushed out to the porch and saw Willard carrying Donny. Charlie leaped off the porch and took Donny into his arms.

"Is he dead?" I asked, clutching at the porch railing.

"He's still breathing. Willard, get on your bike and go for a doctor—either Shaw or Benton—but hurry!"

It took Willard nearly two hours because the two Winnetka doctors were out on calls, but even if they had both been available, it would have made no difference. Donny died that night. He was five years old, and

Willard was thirteen. Nobody knew whether he or Cal had fired that tragic shot.

We didn't go to bed that night. Guy and Linda fell asleep on a large chair. Grandmother Bolté, who was obviously praying, sat in her favorite chair in the corner. Willard and Cal sat together on the bench in front of the fireplace like two stone statues. Neither Charlie nor I could sit still until Donny stopped breathing at ten minutes after one in the morning. Then we sat beside the boys.

"You must not spend the rest of your lives blaming yourselves for what happened," said Charlie, reaching for Willard's hands. "You don't know—nobody knows—who fired that shot, and that's not important anyway. You just have to accept the fact that what's done is done and—"

"And trust in the Lord," said Grandmother Bolté.

Willard continued to stare straight ahead. "I prayed, I prayed as hard as I could, that God would spare Donny from the minute I picked him up until he died. He never did anything bad in his life, but I've done plenty of bad things. I prayed that God would take me instead of him. That would have been much fairer, but he didn't do it."

"It isn't up to us, Will, to judge God," Grandmother Bolté added. "He knows what is best for all of us. Maybe Donny would have suffered a great deal if he had lived."

"I'll never forgive God," said Willard, and then he broke down.

One of the worst parts of the whole sad affair occurred the next day when Father came home. He had been visiting a friend in Chicago, and Charlie telephoned him from Mrs. Willy's candy store. When he saw his grandfather walking fast up Prospect Avenue, Willard went out to meet him.

"Nice kind of boy you are," said Father, and he walked on toward the house. Waiting for him on the porch, I couldn't believe he'd said that.

"Father! It was an accident, and it's just as likely that Cal fired that shot!"

Father shook his head and strode grimly into the house.

It was two months before Father would speak to Willard. Finally at breakfast one day, he said, "I'm going to drive to town this afternoon, Will. Want to come along?"

"Yes sir!"

As they walked out of the dining room together, Father rested his arm casually on Willard's shoulder. "I've missed you, boy," he said.

"I've missed you too," whispered Willard.

Father remained vigorous until his death from a heart attack five years later. He was buried next to Mother, and I missed him for a long time. He was the source of a good deal of my own strength. When the next tragedy struck, however, I was grateful he did not have to endure it.

In 1903, when Willard was a sophomore at Michigan State College, our family was expanded by the addition of Cousin Willard Streeter Bass from Wilton, Maine. Cousin Willard, who had decided he didn't want to go into the shoe business started by his father, had found a teaching job in Chicago after earning his master's degree from Harvard. Charlie was quite ready to have another Willard kin share the Winnetka house, and the two men commuted to the city together. To show his appreciation to all of us, Cousin Willard bought us all tickets to a matinee performance of *Mister Bluebeard* at the Iroquois Theater on Wednesday,

December 30. Developing influenza two days before the show, Cousin Willard gave his ticket to Charlie's brother-in-law, Emory Hall.

It was raining the afternoon of the thirtieth, and we arrived at the theater somewhat late. The curtain had already gone up, and there was a mix-up in the seats so Willard had to sit in the row behind the rest of us, in the first balcony. Linda, at thirteen, had been to the theater only twice before and was enthralled. It was Uncle Emory, the foremost minstrel-show banjoist of his day and thus most familiar with theaters, who first noticed the extra light coming from the left side of the stage. A man in overalls ran out from that side and then ran back. One of the six women on the stage fell over backward and hit her head on the floor. Sparks and smoke started to blow across the stage, and the scenery began to blaze. Someone tried to lower the asbestos curtain, but one end of the roller got stuck halfway down. An actor tried to jump up and catch it, unsuccessfully.

By this time people were jamming the aisles, pushing and shoving and trampling those who had fallen. Somehow the flames had spread from the stage to the second balcony, and people were jumping down into the pit with their clothes blazing.

Linda turned to Guy, who was beside her. "You and Father get Mother out. I'll be all right." Guy nodded, and Uncle Emory shouted that he'd help Linda.

Charlie and Guy got me out through the doorway onto the fire escape platform where I sat clinging to a crossbar until firemen raised a ladder and carried me down. I was not seriously hurt, but I had twisted my good leg in the crush and was taken to a hospital. Charlie, knocked all the way down the iron steps, didn't even notice his bruises as he set out to find the rest of the family. Guy was still on the fire escape platform where Willard found him. For some reason the steps became hopelessly blocked right after Charlie was knocked down. If people had only moved sooner, the thirty or forty whose bodies were found just inside the doorway might have been saved.

Guy and Willard were separated again by the frantic mass of people. Firemen were already carrying burning and blackened bodies out of the theater and laying them in rows on the sidewalks and in stores. Guy tried desperately to find Willard but could see nothing but the equally desperate people around him. He finally decided to go with the throng, and when he was able to break loose, he made his way to Uncle John Willard's house. Willard climbed up on a ladder truck on Randolph Street in hopes of seeing some of the family, or of being seen. Eventually he gave up and went to the Northwestern Depot to wait for some means of transportation home. There Charlie and his brother Anson, who was helping him search, found him. They told him about Guy and me and put him on the train for Winnetka. Then they started touring the nearly one hundred temporary morgues.

They found Uncle Emory's body that night and continued the search for Linda the next day. There were five hundred and seventy-one bodies, more than half of them children. Not until the morning of the third day did they find Linda, in an undertaking establishment far out near the stockyards. She was wrapped in a clean white blanket, and she didn't have a mark on her.

I came home from the hospital that day, and I thought I really couldn't bear this second tragedy. Linda had been so beautiful, and we had started to develop the same kind of relationship that I had with my mother. When I saw how devastated Charlie was, however, I tried to put my own grief aside. Of course he was exhausted after his days of searching, and it had been heartbreaking to see all those other children even before he found Linda. For ten days every flag was at half-mast and every building in downtown Chicago was draped with black and purple. Linda was buried next to Donny, and once again relatives and friends gathered to try to comfort us. This time, however, Charlie was inconsolable. He sat for hours at a time in Linda's room, unwilling—or unable—to respond to his mother's efforts or his sons' or mine to help him.

Cousin Willard shared our grief, but he also felt terribly guilty. When Charlie finally came downstairs, Cousin Willard said, "I know that no words of mine can possibly make any difference, but I have to speak for my own sake. I have an overwhelming feeling of guilt. If I hadn't provided those wretched tickets, your daughter would be alive today. And then not to go myself! What makes me feel the worst is that I'm still alive!"

Momentarily aroused, Charlie said, "All you did was give us a nice Christmas present. What happened had nothing to do with you. Besides, I had intended to buy tickets for the family myself."

"Thank you for that. Now will you come for a walk with me? A little exercise would be good for both of us."

They took a walk, and the next day the two of them took the train into Chicago as usual. Charlie tried to go back to work. For several weeks he went through the motions, but it soon became apparent that he was doing virtually nothing. He would sit at his desk and gaze out the window or draw geometric designs on his order pad. By that time we had a telephone, and Mr. Harmon called me to discuss Charlie's condition. At home he was incapable of making the simplest decision—whether he'd like his morning egg poached or scrambled, for instance.

I tried every reasonable approach I could think of to bring him back to himself, but with no success. Finally I lost my temper and confronted him one evening when we were alone.

"You seem to think you're the only one grieving over the loss of Linda," I said. "How do you think her grandmother feels? And her brothers? How do you think I feel? No family should have to endure two such tragedies as ours, but they happened. And we can't just quit. We have to go on living, if only for Willard and Guy. You've always said you want the best for them, including a college education, but if you don't pull yourself together, you're going to lose your job. Then they'll have to go to work, and that will be the end of your great plans for them. Are you listening to me, Charlie?"

Charlie nodded wearily. "I hear you, and you're not saying anything I haven't said to myself. I'll try, Jessie, I really will, but somehow nothing seems worthwhile."

He did try, but without success, and my prophecy came true. With regret, Sam Harmon called Charlie in and said he would have to leave. "Call it a leave of absence," said Sam. "Come back and see me when you're your old self again."

Guy got a part-time job with a local grocery store, like Charlie years before. Willard got a full-time job for the summer and offered to quit college, but I wouldn't hear of it. Instead I went to work. For years I had been patronizing a dressmaking shop in Winnetka, and when the manager quit in 1904, I applied for the job. The owner may have had some doubts about my business ability, but he was sure I would attract other desirable customers. He hired me, and his assumption proved correct. Willard was able to return to Michigan State for his junior year.

CHAPTER ELEVEN

It is Saturday. I have been in this hospital for a week, and I am thoroughly sick of it. The last time I was here, they kept me for three weeks. Since Charlie was with me most of that time though, I didn't feel so cut off. Jess and Willard come as often as they can, but they're busy living their own lives. The boys are in school, Willard is working hard in his new job with the Reilly Paint Company, and Jess spends all her free time rolling bandages at the Red Cross. When she's at home, she knits socks for our soldiers. I must ask her to bring me some wool. I can knit here as well as anyplace else.

I doze off after lunch and waken suddenly, dreaming that Charlie has come to see me and is holding my hand. When I open my eyes, sure enough, he is standing by my bed and holding my hand. He kisses me and pulls a chair over so he can sit right next to the bed.

"How did you manage to get away?" I ask as he reaches for my hand again.

"Compassionate leave. I may have exaggerated your head injury just a trifle. The commanding officer at the base was very sympathetic and said of course I had to come and see you. He even laid on transport to the train."

"I suppose you had to sit up all night."

"Well, yes, but at least I had a seat. The train was crowded. I did get some sleep, however. Now tell me how you are. You look pretty well, considering."

"I am quite well, considering. The head doesn't hurt at all unless I touch the bruised spot. Most of the time the leg doesn't hurt either. Does Willard know you're here? I'm sure he'd like to see you."

"I called his house from the station. He was still at work, but I had a nice chat with Jess. She said they would come and see you after Willard gets home. I'll take them out to supper, and they'll take me to the station. I have to go back tonight on the nine forty-five."

I was hoping he could spend the night at Willard's, but we have a good visit. Jess thoughtfully lengthens the time he can be with me by bringing a picnic supper, which we all share in the solarium. The boys, as always, are delighted to see their grandfather. I hate to see them all leave, especially Charlie, but I am so tired by the time visiting hours are over that I go to sleep quickly. I dream of trying to catch a train with Charlie and losing him, only to realize he has boarded the train and left without me.

Charlie looks exhausted, and I'm sure he's lost more weight. I know he cares deeply about all those boys in his hospital—and so many of them are dying! I pray the war will end soon so they can all go home and Charlie can perhaps retire. He's worked hard all his life except for that sad time after Linda died. For more than a year I was afraid he wouldn't ever come out of his depression. We had him thoroughly checked by two doctors, but they could find nothing wrong with him physically. His mother, his brother Anson, Cousin Willard, and I all tried to entice him out of his shell, without success.

My job at the dressmaking shop was a lifesaver for me, and not only for the essential income it provided. It got me out of the house and gave me a new interest. Never having had a job before, I was surprised at how hard it is to have to go to work six days a week, even though I liked the work. There's so little time for one's self. The shop closed at noon on Wednesdays, and I treasured those free afternoons. I learned what was required of me in the job easily, and I gradually acquired a degree of patience with the girls I was supervising and the customers. Many of the women who came in to have dresses made were friends of mine, and I felt obliged to tell them when I thought the dresses were unbecoming or didn't fit properly. As a result I spoiled more than one sale. Eventually I learned to be more tactful, expressing my opinion only when it was asked for, and most of the customers came back, saying they appreciated my honesty.

In the meantime Charlie was gradually returning to normal. A year before Linda died, he had met two German Americans from Faribault, Minnesota, who ran a small experimental machine shop in which they were trying to perfect a shadowless arc light. They switched direction when they were approached by a man who wanted a portable gas lighting system for circuses and carnivals. At that time these shows were being lit by gasoline flares, which provided flickering light, used a great deal of gasoline, and posed a serious fire hazard. The experimenters produced a light that satisfied the client and then invented a much better one that they wanted to market. They needed money, however, and they appealed to Charlie. Borrowing money from a bank, Charlie founded a company called Bolté and Weyer, Incorporated, took 50 percent of the stock because he'd put up all the money, and elected himself president and treasurer.

To my relief and joy, he became his old self again, full of vigor and enthusiasm. It was his idea to try to sell the new mantle lights to the Hagenbeck-Wallace Circus, and he sent his partner, George Weyer, to see Ben Wallace at the circus's winter quarters in Peru, Indiana. Even though the light had been designed for the inside of the big top, old Ben insisted that it be tested outdoors in the midst of a blizzard with the temperature below zero. The light went right on glowing even when they pounded the support with a tent stake and even when they threw buckets of water directly on the blazing mantle. When Ben took George Weyer into his office, told him how many lights he would need, and asked what they would cost, George said $2,700, a price that included an extravagant markup. Ben Wallace, who was quite deaf, shook his head and said he would not pay a cent more than $4,500. George gulped twice and said he would provide the lights for that sum if Ben would pay a thousand dollars down to bind the bargain. Ben pulled $1,500 from his pants pocket and gave it to George then and there.

That down payment not only covered the cost of producing Mr. Wallace's lamps but also gave Bolté and Weyer a profit of almost a thousand dollars. The young company proceeded to flood the circus and carnival field with the new lights—at the whopping markup inadvertently approved by Ben Wallace—and cornered the market on repairs because all the parts had special threads and other special features.

The company had another piece of luck in those early days. Charlie and George decided, with business coming in so fast, that they should have enough machinery to do all their own manufacturing. They searched around and found a small chandelier manufacturing shop that had gone bankrupt and bought it for $1,300, about one third the original cost of the engine lathe, speed lathe, screw machine, etc. The owner threw in all the tools and junk around the place, junk that included a lot of brass scraps for which a junkman offered them thirteen cents a pound. George said he could have the lot for $700, but the dealer declined, sticking to thirteen cents a pound. When they started weighing and the total reached $600 before they were halfway through, the dealer tried to revive the $700 offer, but without success. He wound up paying $1,325, covering Bolté and Weyer's new shop plus a twenty-five-dollar profit. As president, Charlie decided to give himself a salary of one hundred dollars a week, and I decided that I could retire from the dressmaking business. I never regretted my two years in the shop, but

I was nearly fifty by then and found that being on my feet as much as I needed to be was very tiring.

Willard was a hard working, reliable young man, but he couldn't seem to stay in one job for long. He really wanted to be a farmer on his own farm, but of course he had no money when he graduated from Michigan State, and Charlie and I had none to spare. Willard tried teaching animal husbandry, first at Utah State College and then at Rhode Island State College. When his salary at Rhode Island was cut from $1,200 to $900 a year, he sent out a flock of letters to other colleges and universities. After a couple of promising prospects fell through, he began to feel desperate. By that time he and Jess were married and had young John. Consequently there was rejoicing in their household when Charlie wrote and invited Willard to go to work for Bolté and Weyer, Incorporated.

Willard, Jess, and John stayed with us in Winnetka for about a month during the summer of 1907, while they were house hunting. We still lived in the big house, with Charlie's mother and Guy, when he was home from college. We were all pleased to have a baby in the house again, especially Jane Bolté, who was entranced by her first great grandchild. All went well for the first two weeks, and then John developed a case of the colic. When his cry turned into a wail, I went into his room and picked him up. Holding him on my shoulder, patting his back, and singing softly, I carried him downstairs to the coolest of the three living rooms. I sat down in the old rocker in which I had rocked my own babies. Before long John was asleep.

Then Jess appeared in the doorway, frowning. "What are you doing with my baby?" she demanded.

"I'm just trying to calm him down so he can get some rest."

"You'll spoil him. He's got to learn that he's not going to be picked up every time he cries."

"He's been crying for more than an hour, and that's not like him. I'm sure he's in pain. And besides, he's only three months old. I don't think a little cuddling will spoil him."

"Mother Bolté, I don't mean to be rude. You're older than I am, and you've had babies of your own, but I'm sure you'll agree that John Henry is my responsibility. I'm going to put him back in his crib now until it's time for him to get up and be fed."

Without another word, I handed the baby over to his mother. He began to cry again the minute he was put down in the crib and continued until Jess deemed it the right time to feed him.

That night I told Charlie about the incident. "I think she was wrong to take him and put him back to bed—he needed comforting—but I respect her for standing up for her rights."

Charlie grinned. "It isn't only your names that are the same. Young Jess is just as independent and just as determined as you've always been. Poor Willard. I hope he'll be able to stand up for his rights."

The house Willard found included not only modern plumbing but also electric lights and a telephone. Jess was very pleased, and John Henry got over his colic. In the course of the next three years, his two brothers were born: Brown (like me, Jess wanted to keep her maiden name in the family), born in 1908, and Charles Guy II, the first (not counting my first) of five boy babies named for Charlie, born in 1910. That was also the year Guy graduated from the University of Michigan. He majored in engineering, but he wasn't really interested in that field, and after a couple of attempts to land engineering jobs, he appealed to Charlie. Charlie was quite ready to hire him to work in the Bolté and Weyer machine shop. Willard had fitted in well and now was about to be left in charge of the company and its thirty other employees.

I had never lost my longing to go around the world. When Charlie and I were married, I had persuaded him to promise that we would make the trip if we ever had the money. Now, thanks to the success of the lamp company and to my inheritance from Father, we had more than enough. I could hardly believe it was true, but we set out for California by train on September 1, 1910.

Afterward

When Woodrow Wilson decided it was time for the United States to help England and France fight the Germans in World War I, my father, Guy Willard Bolté, joined the army. By that time he had his bachelor's degree in engineering, having attended the University of Michigan, Michigan State, the Massachusetts Institute of Technology, and once again Michigan State. The recruiting officer wanted him to sign on as an engineer, but Guy refused, having no interest in the subject.

He was then told that if he continued to refuse, he would still be accepted as a second lieutenant, but he would never be promoted. That suited Pappy (as he later chose to be called) just fine. His brother Willard wanted to enlist too, but by that time he had three small boys and wouldn't be able to support them on a soldier's pay—even an officer's.

Since Jessie had inherited money from her father, however, my grandfather, Charles Guy Bolté the first, decided he could do something to help "save the world for democracy." He was put in charge of the Great Lakes Training Station where thousands of American young men learned to be sailors.

In his book, *Bolté Memoirs and Genealogy*, Uncle Willard says nothing about his father's job except to report his grief over the death of hundreds of boys killed by the flu epidemic. When Charles Guy came home at the end of the war, he was worn out and died only a few months later.

Guy, on the other hand, seems to have had an easier time, even though he really was "in the trenches." Willard's book included a number of Pappy's letters. Of course, my father omitted the grimmer details, but he always considered his enlistment the "great adventure" of his life. Just before his death, he said, "This is a helluva way for a soldier to die."

Even though her men had not yet come home, Willard wrote that his "little mother" took a cab from Winnetka into Chicago to join the celebration of the end of the war.

Some months before he went to France, Guy met Mary Stuart, a young woman whose first husband had deserted her, leaving her with Alan, a boy born in 1909. Guy and Mary were married before he sailed. I don't think Jessie was very happy about their union, though in her only known comment she wrote Guy that she was happy his bride was not pregnant.

Somewhere along the line Jessie acquired the nickname Byma, and that's what she was called by relatives of all ages. My mother took my brother Chuck and me to Florida to spend six weeks with Byma when I was five and six. She was then living in the Oaks Hotel in Daytona. It rained almost every day that first year, so Mother often took us to the movies. Byma did not approve, but what else can you do with a five-year-old and a nine-year-old? No TV in those days, of course, and books and cards got boring eventually. During the second visit, we were enrolled at the local school. All I remember about that is drawing endless zeroes.

Byma was critical of our table manners too. She scolded me for putting sugar on my lettuce and tomato salad, even though my father did that too. She also said she was "shocked" when I put a whole potato in my mouth at once.

Later Mother comforted me by saying, "It was a very small potato."

Byma came to visit us at the Lexington Avenue house in Connecticut several times. She used to play popular tunes rather thumpingly on the piano. It occurs to me now that she probably couldn't reach the pedals.

She came to Cuckoo Manor (Pappy's name for our new house) only once. I have a hazy memory of a quarrel between her and Janet, my stepmother, but I am not sure that really happened.

Byma and I had one conversation in which she told me that my mother had urged my father to remarry after she died when I was eleven.

Eventually Byma moved to Mobile, Alabama, where she died when I was fourteen. My father went to her funeral of course. I remember being alone in the house and playing "None But the Lonely Heart" on the piano.

I didn't know most of the details of Byma's life until I read Uncle Willard's book years later. She truly was the epitome of my mantra: "Courage and fortitude."

ABOUT THE AUTHOR

Linda Bolté Whitlock

Linda Bolté Whitlock was born in 1923 in Greenwich, Connecticut. After graduating Wellesley College with a bachelor's degree in English, she married Victor Whitlock in 1946 and went on to have three daughters, seven grandchildren, and five great-grandchildren so far.

Throughout her career, Whitlock has taught English at the Greenwich Academy, Wilbraham Academy, and The Williams School—where she retired as dean of students. Currently she resides in Arlington, Virginia.

Made in the USA
Charleston, SC
09 April 2015